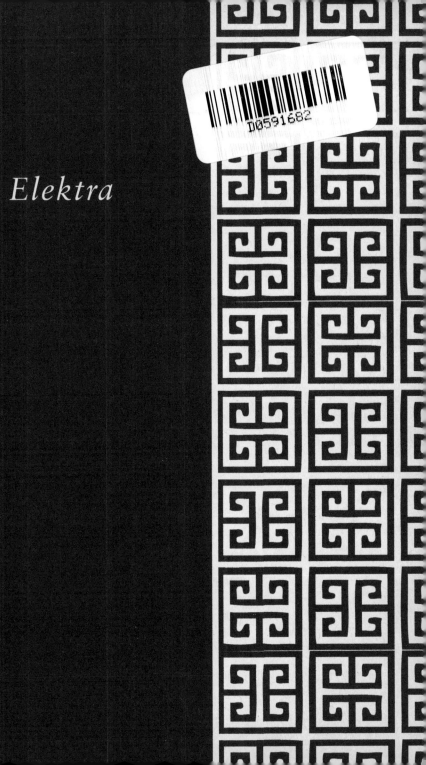

Elektra

ALSO BY ROBERT BAGG

Madonna of the Cello: Poems (Wesleyan University Press)

Euripides' Hippolytos (Oxford University Press)

The Scrawny Sonnets and Other Narratives
(Illinois University Press)

Euripides' The Bakkhai (University of Massachusetts Press)

Sophocles' Oedipus the King
(University of Massachusetts Press)

Body Blows: Poems New and Selected
(University of Massachusetts Press)

The Oedipus Plays of Sophocles with Notes and Introductions by Robert
and Mary Bagg (University of Massachusetts Press)

Niké and Other Poems (Azul Editions)

HORSEGOD: Collected Poems (iUniverse)

Euripides III: Hippolytos and Other Plays
(Oxford University Press)

The Tandem Ride and Other Excursions
(Spiritus Mundi Press)

The Complete Plays of Sophocles with James Scully
(Harper Perennial)

The Oedipus Cycle
(Harper Perennial)

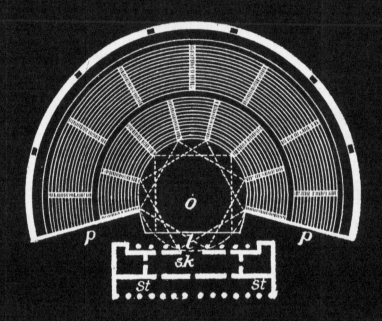

ELEKTRA

A New Translation by Robert Bagg

SOPHOCLES

HARPER ● PERENNIAL

NEW YORK ● LONDON ● TORONTO ● SYDNEY ● NEW DELHI ● AUCKLAND

HARPER ● PERENNIAL

For performance rights to *Elektra* contact The Strothman Agency, LLC, at 197 Eighth Street, Flagship Wharf – 611, Charlestown, MA 02129, or by email at info@strothmanagency.com.

HarperCollins books may be purchased for educational, business, or sales promotional use. For information, please e-mail the Special Markets Department at SPsales@harpercollins.com.

FIRST EDITION

Designed by Justin Dodd

Library of Congress Cataloging-in-Publication Data is available upon request.

ISBN 978-0-06-213206-2

14 15 16 /RRD 10 9 8 7 6 5 4 3

For Ralph Lee, who drew me into a lifetime
of translating Greek drama by staging my version of Euripides' Kyklops
at Amherst College in November 1956

CONTENTS

WHEN THEATER WAS LIFE: THE WORLD OF SOPHOCLES

I

Greek theater emerged from the same explosive creativity that propelled the institutions and ways of knowing of ancient Athens, through two and a half millennia, into our own era. These ranged from the concept and practice of democracy, to an aggressive use of logic with few holds barred, to a philosophy singing not of gods and heroes but of what exists, where it came from, and why. Athenians distinguished history from myth, acutely observed the human form, and reconceived medicine from a set of beliefs and untheorized practices into a science.

Playwrights, whose work was presented to audiences of thousands, effectively took center stage as critics and interpreters of their own culture. Athenian drama had one major showing each year at the nine-day Festival of Dionysos. It was rigorously vetted. Eight dramatists (three tragedians, five comic playwrights), chosen in open competition, were "granted choruses," a down-to-earth term meaning that the city financed production of their plays. For the Athenians theater was as central to civic life as the assembly, law courts, temples, and agora.

Historians summing up Athens' cultural importance have tended to emphasize its glories, attending less to the brutal institutions and policies that underwrote the city's wealth and dominance: its slaves, for instance, who worked the mines that enriched the communal treasury; or its policy of executing the men and enslaving the women and children of enemy cities that refused to surrender on demand. During its long war with Sparta, Athens' raw and unbridled democracy became increasingly reckless, cruel, and eventually self-defeating. Outside the assembly's daily debates on war, peace, and myriad other issues, Athenian citizens, most notably the indefatigable Socrates, waged ongoing critiques of the city's actions and principles. Playwrights, whom the Athenians called *didaskaloi* (educators), were expected to enlighten audiences about themselves, both individually and collectively. As evidenced by the thirty-three plays that survive, these works presented a huge audience annually with conflicts and dilemmas of the most extreme sort.

To some extent all Sophocles' plays engage personal, social, and political crises and confrontations—not just those preserved in heroic legend but those taking place in his immediate world. Other Athenian intellectuals, including Thucydides, Aeschylus, Euripides, Plato, and Aristophanes, were part of that open-ended discussion in which everything was subject to question, including the viability of the city and its democracy (which was twice voted temporarily out of existence).

II

To this day virtually every Athenian theatrical innovation—from paraphernalia such as scenery, costumes, and masks to the architecture of stage and seating and, not least, to the use of drama as a powerful means of cultural and political commentary—remains in use. We thus inherit from Athens the vital *potential* for drama to engage our realities and to support or critique prevailing orthodoxies.

The myths that engaged Sophocles' audience originated in Homer's epics of the Trojan War and its aftermath. Yet Homer's world was tribal. That of the Greek tragedians was not, or only nominally so. With few exceptions (e.g., Aeschylus' *The Persians*), those playwrights were writing *through* the Homeric world to address, and deal with, the *polis* world they themselves were living in. Sophocles was appropriating stories and situations from these epics, which were central to the mythos of Athenian culture, and re-visioning them into dramatic *agons* (contests) relevant to the tumultuous, often vicious politics of Greek life in the fifth century BCE. Today some of Sophocles' concerns, and the way he approached them, correspond at their deepest levels to events and patterns of thought and conduct that trouble our own time. For example, "[Sophocles'] was an age when war was endemic. And Athens in the late fifth century BC appeared to have a heightened taste for conflict. One year of two in the Democratic Assembly, Athenian citizens voted in favor of military aggression" (Hughes, 138).

Each generation interprets and translates these plays in keeping with the style and idiom it believes best suited for tragedy.

Inevitably even the most skilled at preserving the original's essentials, while attuning its voice to the present, will eventually seem the relic of a bygone age. We have assumed that a contemporary translation should attempt to convey not only what the original seems to have been communicating, but *how* it communicated—not in its saying, only, but in its *doing*. It cannot be said too often: these plays were social and historical *events* witnessed by thousands in a context and setting infused with religious ritual and civic protocol. They were not transitory, one-off entertainments but were preserved, memorized, and invoked. Respecting this basic circumstance will not guarantee a successful translation, but it is a precondition for giving these works breathing room in which their strangeness, their rootedness in distinct historical moments, can flourish. As with life itself, they were not made of words alone.

Athenian playwrights relied on a settled progression of scene types: usually a prologue followed by conversations or exchanges in which situations and attitudes are introduced, then a series of confrontations that feature cut-and-thrust dialogue interrupted by messenger narratives, communal songs of exultation or grieving, and less emotionally saturated, or 'objective,' choral odes that respond to or glance off the action. Audiences expected chorus members to be capable of conveying the extraordinary range of expressive modes, from the pithy to the operatic, that Sophocles had at his disposal. To translate this we have needed the resources not only of idiomatic English but also of rhetorical gravitas and, on occasion, colloquial English. Which is why we have adopted, regarding vocabulary and 'levels of speech,' a wide and varied palette. When Philoktetes exclaims, "You said it, boy," that saying corresponds in character to the colloquial Greek expression. On the other hand Aias's "Long rolling waves of time . . ." is as elevated, without being pompous, as anything can be.

Unfortunately we've been taught, and have learned to live with, washed-out stereotypes of the life and art of 'classical' times—just as we have come to associate Greek sculpture with the color of its underlying material, usually white marble. The classical historian Bettany Hughes writes in *The Hemlock Cup* (81) that temples and monuments were painted or stained in "Technicolor" to be seen under the bright Attic sun. The statues' eyes were not blanks gazing off into space. They had color: a *look*. To restore their flesh tones, their eye color, and the bright hues of their cloaks would seem a desecration. We should understand that this is so—even as we recognize that, for us, there is no going back. We've been conditioned to preserve not the reality of ancient Greek sculpture in its robust cultural ambience and physical setting, but our own fixed conception of it as colorless and sedate—a perception created, ironically, by the weathering and ravages of centuries. No one can change that. Still, as translators we have a responsibility not to reissue a stereotype of classical Greek culture but rather to recoup, to the extent possible, the vitality of its once living reality.

Regarding its highly inflected language, so different from our more context-driven modern English, we recognize that locutions sounding contorted, coy, recondite, or annoyingly roundabout were a feature of ordinary Greek and were intensified in theatrical discourse. Highly wrought, larger-than-life expressions, delivered without artificial amplification to an audience of thousands, did not jar when resonating in the vast Theater of Dionysos, but may to our own Anglophone ears when delivered from our more intimate stages and screens, or read in our books and electronic tablets. Accordingly, where appropriate, and especially in rapid exchanges, we have our characters speak more straightforwardly—as happens in Greek stichomythia, when characters argue back and forth in alternating lines (or 'rows') of verse, usually linked by a word they hold in common. Here, for example, is a snippet from *Aias* (1305–1309)[1] that pivots on "right," "killer," "dead" and "god(s)":

TEUKROS   A righteous cause is my courage.
MENELAOS What? It's right to defend my killer?
TEUKROS   Your killer!? You're dead? And still alive?
MENELAOS A god saved me. But he *wanted* me dead.
TEUKROS   If the gods saved you, why disrespect them?

There are no rules for determining when a more-literal or less-literal approach is appropriate. Historical and dramatic context have to be taken into account. The objective is not only to render the textual meaning (which is ordinarily more on the phrase-by-phrase than the word-by-word level) but also to communicate the feel and impact embedded in that meaning. Dictionaries are indispensable for translators, but they are not sufficient. The meanings of words are immeasurably more nuanced and wide-ranging in life than they can ever be in a lexicon. As in life, where most 'sayings' cannot be fully grasped apart from their timing and their place in both personal and social contexts, so in theater: dramatic context must take words up and finish them off. In *Aias*, Teukros, the out-of-wedlock half brother of Aias, and Menelaos, co-commander of the Greek forces, are trading insults. When Menelaos says, "The archer, far from blood dust, thinks he's something," Teukros quietly rejoins, "I'm very good at what I do" (1300–1301).

Understanding the exchange between the two men requires that the reader or audience recognize the 'class' implications of archery. Socially and militarily, archers rank low in the pecking order. They stand to the rear of the battle formation. Archers are archers usually because they can't afford the armor one needs to be a hoplite, a frontline fighter. The point is that Teukros refuses to accept 'his place' in the social and military order. For a Greek audience, the sheer fact of standing his ground against a commander had to have been audacious. But that is not how it automatically registers in most modern word-by-word translations, which tend to make Teukros sound defensive (a trait wholly out of his character in this play). Examples: (a) "Even so, 'tis no sordid craft that I possess," (b) "I'm not the master of a menial skill," (c) "My archery is no contemptible science," (d) "The art I practice is no mean one." These translations are technically accurate. They're scrupulous in reproducing the Greek construction whereby, in an idiomatic context, a negative may register as an assertion—or even, framed as a negative future question, become a command. But tonally, in modern English idiom, Teukros' negation undercuts his assertion (the 'I'm not . . . but even so' formula). To our ears it admits weakness or defensiveness. "I'm very good at what I do," however, is a barely veiled threat. The dramatic arc of the encounter, which confirms that Teukros will not back down for anything or anyone, not even a commander of the Greek army, substantiates that Sophocles meant it to be heard as such.

Hearing the line in context we realize instantly not only what the words are saying but, more pointedly and feelingly, what they're doing. His words are not just 'about' something. They are an act in themselves—not, as in the more literal translations, a duress-driven apologia. Translation must thus respond to an individual character's ever-changing demeanor and circumstance. The speaker's state of mind should show through his or her words, just as in life. Idiomatic or colloquial expressions fit many situations better—especially those that have a more finely tuned emotional economy—than phrases that, if uninhabited, hollowed out, or just plain buttoned-up, sound evasive or euphemistic. Many of the speeches Sophocles gives his characters are as abrupt and common as he might himself have spoken to his fellow Athenians in the assembly, in the agora, to his troops, his actors, or his family.

At times we have chosen a more literal translation in passages where scholars have opted for a seemingly more accessible modern phrase. At the climactic moment in *Oedipus the King*, when Oedipus realizes he has killed his father and fathered children with his mother, he says in a modern prose version by Hugh Lloyd-Jones: "Oh, oh! All is now clear. O light, may I now look on you for the last time, I who am revealed as cursed in my birth, cursed in my marriage, cursed in my killing!" (Greek 1182–1885). When Lloyd-Jones uses and repeats the word "cursed," he is compressing a longer Greek phrase meaning "being shown to have done what must not be done." This compression shifts the emphasis from his unsuspecting human

actions toward the realm of the god who acted to "curse" him.
The following lines keep the original grammatical construction:

> All! All! It has all happened!
> It was all true. O light! Let this
> be the last time I look on you.
> You see now who I am—
> the child who must not be born!
> I loved where I must not love!
> I killed where I must not kill! (1336–1342)

Here Oedipus names the three acts of interfamilial trans-
gression that it was both his good and his ill fortune to have
survived, participated in, and inflicted—birth, sexual love, and
murder in self-defense—focusing not only on the curse each act
has become but now realizing the full and horrific consequence
of each action that was, as it happened, unknowable. Register-
ing the shudder rushing through him, Oedipus's exclamations
convey the shock of his realization: *I did these things without
feeling their horror as I do now.*

Finally, translations tend to be more or less effective depend-
ing on their ability to convey the emotional and physiological
reactions that will give a reader or an audience a kinesthetic re-
lationship to the dramatic moment, whether realized as text or
performance. This is a precondition for maintaining the tactil-
ity that characterizes any living language. Dante wrote that the
spirit of poetry abounds "in the tangled constructions and de-
fective pronunciations" of vernacular speech where language is
renewed and transformed. We have not attempted that—these

are translations, not new works—but we have striven for a language that is spontaneous and generative as opposed to one that is studied and bodiless. We have also worked to preserve the root meaning of Sophocles' Greek, especially his always illuminating metaphors.

III

Sophocles reveals several recurrent attitudes in his plays—sympathy for fate's victims, hostility toward leaders who abuse their power, skepticism toward self-indulgent 'heroes,' disillusionment with war and revenge—that are both personal and politically significant. All his plays to a greater or lesser degree focus on outcasts from their communities. Historically, those who transgress a community's values have either been physically exiled or stigmatized by sanctions and/or shunning. To keep a polity from breaking apart, everyone, regardless of social standing, must abide by certain enforceable communal expectations. Athens in the fifth century BCE practiced political ostracism, a procedure incorporated in its laws. By voting to ostracize a citizen, Athens withdrew its protection and civic benefits—sometimes to punish an offender, but also as a kind of referee's move, expelling a divisive public figure from the city (and from his antagonists) so as to promote a ten-year period of relative peace.

In earlier eras Greek cities also cast out those who committed sacrilege. Murderers of kin, for instance, or blasphemers of a god—in myth and in real life—were banished from Greek cities until the 'unclean' individual 'purged' his crime according to current religious custom. The imperative to banish a kin violator runs so deep that Oedipus, after discovering he has committed patricide and incest, passes judgment on himself and demands to live in exile. In *Oedipus at Kolonos*, he and Antigone have been exiled from Thebes against their will. In the non-Oedipus plays the title characters Philoktetes, Elektra, and Aias, as well as Herakles in *Women of Trakhis*, are not outcasts in the traditional sense, though all have actively or involuntarily offended their social units in some way. They may or may not be typical tragic characters; nonetheless none 'fit' the world they're given to live in. In these translations we've incorporated awareness of social dimensions in the original texts, which, as they involve exercises of power, are no less political than social.

In each of the four non-Oedipus plays, a lethal confrontation or conflict 'crazes' the surface coherence of a society (presumed to be Athenian society, either in itself or as mediated through a military context), thus revealing and heightening its internal contradictions.

In *Women of Trakhis* the revered hero Herakles, when he tries to impose a young concubine on his wife Deianeira, provokes her to desperate measures that unwittingly cause him horrific pain, whereupon he exposes his savage and egomaniacal nature, lashing out at everyone around him, exercising a hero's prerogatives so savagely that he darkens his own reputation and drives his wife to suicide and his son to bitter resentment.

Elektra exposes the dehumanizing cost of taking revenge, by revealing the neurotic, materialistic, and cold-blooded character of the avengers. In *Aias*, when the Greek Army's most powerful soldier tries to assassinate his commanders, whose authority

rests on dubious grounds, he exposes not only them but his own
growing obsolescence in a prolonged war that has more need of
strategic acumen, as exemplified by Odysseus, than brute force.
In *Philoktetes* the title character, abandoned on a deserted is-
land because of a stinking wound his fellow warriors can't live
with, is recalled to active service with the promise of a cure
and rehabilitation. The army needs him and his bow to win the
war. It is a call he resists, until the god Herakles negotiates a
resolution—not in the name of justice, but because Philoktetes'
compliance is culturally mandated. As in *Aias*, the object is to
maintain the integrity and thus the survival of the society itself.
The greatest threat is not an individual's death, which here is
not the preeminent concern, but the disintegration of a society.

In our own time aspects of *Aias* and *Philoktetes* have been
used for purposes that Sophocles, who was the sponsor in Ath-
ens of a healing cult, might have appreciated. Both heroes, but
especially Aias, have been appropriated as exemplars of post-
traumatic stress disorder, in particular as suffered by soldiers
in and out of a war zone. Excerpts from these two plays have
been performed around the United States for veterans, soldiers
on active duty, their families, and concerned others. Ultimately,
however, Sophocles is intent on engaging and resolving inter-
nal contradictions that threaten the historical continuity, the
very future, of the Athenian city-state. He invokes the class con-
tradictions Athens was experiencing by applying them to the
mythical/historical eras from which he draws his plots.

Modern-day relevancies implicit in Sophocles' plays will
come sharply into focus or recede from view depending on
time and circumstance. The constant factors in these plays will

always be their consummate poetry, dramatic propulsion, and the intensity with which they illuminate human motivation and morality. Scholars have also identified allusions in his plays to events in Athenian history. The plague in *Oedipus the King* is described in detail so vivid it dovetails in many respects with Thucydides' more clinical account of the plague that killed one-third to one-half of Athens' population beginning in 429 BCE. Kreon, Antigone's antagonist, displays the imperviousness to rational advice and lack of foresight exhibited by the politicians of Sophocles' era, whose follies Thucydides narrates, and which Sophocles himself was called in to help repair—specifically by taking a democracy that in a fit of imperial overreach suffered, in 413, a catastrophic defeat on the shores of Sicily, and replacing it with a revanchist oligarchy. When Pisander, one of the newly empowered oligarchs, asked Sophocles if he was one of the councilors who had approved the replacement of the democratic assembly by what was, in effect, a junta of four hundred, Sophocles admitted that he had. "Why?" asked Pisander. "Did you not think this a terrible decision?" Sophocles agreed it was. "So weren't you doing something terrible?" "That's right. There was no better alternative." (Aristotle, Rh. 1419a). The lesson? When life, more brutally than drama, delivers its irreversible calamities and judgments, it forces a polity, most movingly, to an utterly unanticipated, wholly 'other' moral and spiritual level.

In *Oedipus at Kolonos* Sophocles alludes to his city's decline when he celebrates a self-confident Athens that no longer existed when Sophocles wrote that play. He gives us Theseus, a throwback to the type of thoughtful, decisive, all-around leader Athens lacked as it pursued policies that left it impoverished and defenseless—this under the delusion that its only enemies were Spartans and Sparta's allies.

IV

Archaeologists have identified scores of local theaters all over the Greek world—stone semicircles, some in cities and at religious destinations, others in rural villages. Within many of these structures both ancient and modern plays are still staged. Hillsides whose slopes were wide and gentle enough to seat a crowd made perfect settings for dramatic encounters and were the earliest theaters. Ancient roads that widened below a gentle hillside, or level ground at a hill's base, provided suitable performance spaces. Such sites, along with every city's agora and a temple dedicated to Dionysos or another god, were the main arenas of community activity. Stone tablets along roads leading to theaters commemorated local victors: athletes, actors, playwrights, singers, and the winning plays' producers. Theaters, in every sense, were open to all the crosscurrents of civic and domestic life.

The components of the earliest theaters reflect their rural origins and were later incorporated into urban settings. *Theatron*, the root of our word "theater," translates as "viewing place" and designated the curved and banked seating area. *Orchestra* was literally "the place for dancing." The costumed actors emerged from and retired to the *skenê*, a word that originally meant, and literally was in the rural theaters, a tent. As theaters evolved to become more permanent structures, the *skenê* developed as well into a "stage building" whose painted facade changed, like a mask, with the characters' various habitats. Depending on the drama, the *skenê* could assume the appearance of a king's grand palace, the Kyklops' cave, a temple to a god, or (reverting to its original material form) an army commander's tent.

Greek drama itself originated in two earlier traditions, one rural, one civic. Choral singing of hymns to honor Dionysos or other gods and heroes, which had begun in the countryside, evolved into the structured choral ode. The costumes and the dancing of choral singers, often accompanied by a reed instrument, are depicted on sixth-century vases that predate the plays staged in the Athenian theater. The highly confrontational nature of every play suggests how early choral odes and dialogues came into being in concert with a fundamental aspect of democratic governance: public and spirited debate. Two or more characters facing off in front of an audience was a situation at the heart of both drama and democratic politics.

Debate, the democratic Athenian art practiced and perfected by politicians, litigators, and thespians—relished and judged by voters, juries, and audiences—flourished in theatrical venues and permeated daily Athenian life. Thucydides used it to narrate his history of the war between Athens and Sparta. He recalled scores of lengthy debates that laid out the motives of politicians, generals, and diplomats as each argued his case for a particular policy or a strategy. Plato, recognizing the open-ended, exploratory power of spirited dialogue, wrote his philosophy entirely in dramatic form.

The Greeks were addicted to contests and turned virtually every chance for determining a winner into a formal competition. The Great Dionysia for playwrights and choral singers and the Olympics for athletes are only the most famous and familiar. The verbal *agon* remains to this day a powerful medium for testing and judging issues. And character, as in the debate between Teukros and Menelaos, may be laid bare. But there is no guarantee. Persuasiveness can be, and frequently is, manipulative (e.g., many of the sophists evolved into hired rhetorical guns, as distinguished from the truth-seeking, pre-Socratic philosophers). Sophocles may well have had the sophists' amorality in mind when he had Odysseus persuade Neoptomolos that betraying Philoktetes would be a patriotic act and bring the young man fame.

Though they were part of a high-stakes competition, the plays performed at the Dionysia were part of a religious ceremony whose chief purpose was to honor theater's patron god, Dionysos. The god's worshippers believed that Dionysos' powers and rituals transformed the ways in which they experienced and dealt with their world—from their enthralled response to theatrical illusion and disguise to the exhilaration, liberation, and violence induced by wine. Yet the festival also aired, or licensed, civic issues that might otherwise have had no truly public, *polis*-wide expression. The playwrights wrote as *politai*, civic poets, as distinguished from those who focused on personal lyrics and shorter choral works. Though *Aias* and *Philoktetes* are set in a military milieu, the issues they engage are essentially civil and political. Neither *Aias* nor *Philoktetes* is concerned with the 'enemy of record,' Troy, but rather with Greek-on-Greek conflict. With civil disruption, and worse. In fact one need look no further than the play venue itself for confirmation

of the interpenetration of the civic with the military—a concern
bordering on preoccupation—when, every year, the orphans of
warriors killed in battle were given new hoplite armor and a
place of honor at the Festival of Dionysos.

Communal cohesiveness and the historical continuity of the
polity are most tellingly threatened from within: in *Aias* by the
individualistic imbalance and arrogance of Aias, whose warrior
qualities and strengths are also his weakness—they lead him
to destroy the war spoil that is the common property of the en-
tire Greek army—and in *Philoktetes* by the understandable and
just, yet inordinately unyielding, self-preoccupation of Philok-
tetes himself. In both cases the fundamental, encompassing
question is this: With what understandings, what basic values,
is the commonality of the *polis* to be recovered and rededicated
in an era in which civic cohesiveness is under the extreme pres-
sure of a war Athens is losing (especially at the time *Philoktetes*
was produced) and, further, the simmering stasis of unresolved
class or caste interests? In sharply different ways, all three plays
of the Oedipus cycle, as well as *Aias* and *Elektra*, cast doubt
on the legitimacy of usurped, authoritarian, or publicly disap-
proved leadership.

Given the historical and political dynamism of these great,
instructive works, we've aimed to translate and communicate
their challenge to Athenian values for a contemporary audience
whose own values are no less under duress.

V

The Great Dionysia was the central and most widely attended event of the political year, scheduled after winter storms had abated so that foreign visitors could come and bear witness to Athens' wealth, civic pride, imperial power, and artistic imagination. For eight or nine days each spring, during the heyday of Greek theater in the fifth century BCE, Athenians flocked to the temple grounds sacred to Dionysos on the southern slope of the Acropolis. After dark on the first day, a parade of young men hefted a giant phallic icon of the god from the temple and into the nearby theater. As the icon had been festooned with garlands of ivy and a mask of the god's leering face, their raucous procession initiated a dramatic festival called the City Dionysia, a name that differentiated it from the festival's ancient rural origins in Dionysian myth and cult celebrations of the god. As the festival gained importance in the sixth century BCE, most likely through the policies of Pisistratus, it was also known as the Great Dionysia.

Pisistratus, an Athenian tyrant in power off and on beginning in 561 BCE and continuously from 546 to 527, had good reason for adapting the Rural Dionysia as Athens' Great Dionysia: "Dionysos was a god for the 'whole' of democratic Athens" (Hughes, 213). Everyone, regardless of political faction or social standing, could relate to the boisterous communal activities of the festival honoring Dionysos: feasting, wine drinking, dancing, singing, romping through the countryside, and performing or witnessing dithyrambs and more elaborate dramatic works. The Great Dionysia thus served to keep in check, if not transcend, internal factionalizing by giving all citizens a 'natural' stake in Athens—Athens not simply as a place but as a venerable polity with ancient cultural roots. To this end Pisistratus had imported from Eleutherai an ancient phallic representation of Dionysos, one that took several men to carry.

Lodged as it was in a temple on the outskirts of Athens, this bigger-than-life icon gave the relatively new, citified cult the sanctified air of hoary antiquity (Csapo and Slater, 103–104). Thus validated culturally, the Great Dionysia was secured as a host to reassert, and annually rededicate, Athens as a democratic polity. As Bettany Hughes notes in *The Hemlock Cup*, "to call Greek drama an 'art-form' is somewhat anachronistic. The Greeks (unlike many modern-day bureaucrats) didn't distinguish drama as 'art'—something separate from 'society,' 'politics,' [or] 'life.' Theater was fundamental to democratic Athenian business. . . . [In] the fifth century this was the place where Athenian democrats came to understand the very world they lived in" (Hughes, 213).

The occasion offered Athens the chance to display treasure exacted from subjugated 'allies' (or tributes others willingly brought to the stage) and to award gold crowns to citizens whose achievements Athens' leaders wished to honor. Theater attendance itself was closely linked to citizenship; local town councils issued free festival passes to citizens in good standing. The ten generals elected yearly to conduct Athens' military campaigns poured libations to Dionysos. The theater's bowl seethed with a heady, sometimes unruly brew of military, political, and religious energy.

Performances began at dawn and lasted well into the

afternoon. The 14,000 or more Athenians present watched in god knows what state of anticipation or anxiety. Whatever else it did to entertain, move, and awe, Athenian tragedy consistently exposed human vulnerability to the gods' malice and favoritism. Because the gods were potent realities to Athenian audiences, they craved and expected an overwhelming emotional, physically distressing experience. That expectation distinguishes the greater intensity with which Athenians responded to plays from our own less challenging, more routine and frequent encounters with drama. Athenians wept while watching deities punish the innocent or unlucky, a reaction that distressed Plato. In his *Republic*, rather than question the motives or morality of the all-powerful Olympian gods for causing mortals grief, he blamed the poets and playwrights for their unwarranted wringing of the audience's emotions. He held that the gods had no responsibility for human suffering. True to form, Plato banned both poets and playwrights from his ideal city.

Modern audiences would be thoroughly at home with other, more cinematic stage effects. The sights and sounds tragedy delivered in the Theater of Dionysos were often spectacular. Aristotle, who witnessed a lifetime of productions in the fourth century—well after Sophocles' own lifetime, when the plays were performed in the heat of their historical moment—identified "spectacle," or *opsis*, as one of the basic (though to him suspect) elements of tragic theater. Under the influence of Aristotle, who preferred the study to the stage, and who therefore emphasized the poetry rather than the production of works, ancient commentators tended to consider "the visual aspects of drama [as] both vulgar and archaic" (Csapo and Slater, 257).

Nonetheless, visual and aural aspects there were: oboe music; dancing and the singing of set-piece odes by a chorus; masks that transformed the same male actor, for instance, into a swarthy-faced young hero, a dignified matron, Argos with a hundred eyes, or the Kyklops with only one. The theater featured painted scenery and large-scale constructions engineered with sliding platforms and towering cranes. It's hardly surprising that Greek tragedy has been considered a forerunner of Italian opera.

Judges awarding prizes at the Great Dionysia were chosen by lot from a list supplied by the council—one judge from each of Athens' ten tribes. Critical acumen was not required to get one's name on the list, but the *choregoi* (the producers and financial sponsors of the plays) were present when the jury was assembled and probably had a hand in its selection. At the conclusion of the festival the ten selected judges, each having sworn that he hadn't been bribed or unduly influenced, would inscribe on a tablet the names of the three competing playwrights in descending order of merit. The rest of the process depended on chance. The ten judges placed their ballots in a large urn. The presiding official drew five at random, counted up the weighted vote totals, and declared the winner.

VI

When Sophocles was a boy, masters trained him to excel in music, dance, and wrestling. He won crowns competing against his age-mates in all three disciplines. Tradition has it that he first appeared in Athenian national life at age fifteen, dancing naked (according to one source) and leading other boy dancers in a hymn of gratitude to celebrate Athens' defeat of the Persian fleet in the straits of Salamis.

Sophocles' father, Sophroniscus, manufactured weapons and armor (probably in a factory operated by slaves), and his mother, Phaenarete, was a midwife. The family lived in Kolonos, a rural suburb just north of Athens. Although his parents were not aristocrats, as most other playwrights' were, they surely had money and owned property; thus their status did not hamper their son's career prospects. Sophocles' talents as a dramatist, so formidable and so precociously developed, won him early fame. As an actor he triumphed in his own now-lost play, *Nausicaä*, in the role of the eponymous young princess who discovers the nearly naked Odysseus washed up on the beach while playing ball with her girlfriends.

During Sophocles' sixty-five-year career as a *didaskalos* he wrote and directed more than 120 plays and was awarded first prize at least eighteen times. No record exists of his placing lower than second. Of the seven entire works of his that survive, along with a substantial fragment of a satyr play, *The Trackers*, only two very late plays can be given exact production dates: *Philoktetes* in 409 and *Oedipus at Kolonos,* staged posthumously in 401. Some evidence suggests that *Antigone* was produced around 442–441 and *Oedipus the King* in the 420s. *Aias, Elektra*, and *Women of Trakhis* have been conjecturally, but never conclusively, dated through stylistic analysis. Aristotle, who had access we forever lack to the hundreds of fifth-century plays produced at the Dionysia, preferred Sophocles to his rivals Aeschylus and Euripides. He considered *Oedipus the King* the perfect example of tragic form, and developed his theory of tragedy from his analysis of it.

Sophocles' fellow citizens respected him sufficiently to vote him into high city office on at least three occasions. He served for a year as chief tribute-collector for Athens' overseas empire. A controversial claim by Aristophanes of Byzantium, in the third century, implies that Sophocles' tribe was so impressed by a production of *Antigone* that they voted him in as one of ten military generals (*strategoi*) in 441–440. Later in life Sophocles was respected as a participant in democratic governance at the highest level. In 411 he was elected to a ten-man commission charged with replacing Athens' discredited democratic governance with an oligarchy, a development that followed the military's catastrophic defeat in Sicily in 413.

Most ancient biographical sources attest to Sophocles' good looks, his easygoing manner, and his enjoyment of life. Athanaeus' multivolume *Deipnosophistai*, a compendium of gossip and dinner chat about and among ancient worthies, includes several vivid passages that reveal Sophocles as both a commanding presence and an impish prankster, ready one moment to put down a schoolmaster's boorish literary criticism and the next to flirt with the wine boy.

Sophocles is also convincingly described as universally respected, with amorous inclinations and intensely religious qualities that, to his contemporaries, did not seem incompatible. Religious piety meant something quite different to an Athenian than the humility, sobriety, and aversion to sensual pleasure it might suggest to us—officially, if not actually. His involvement in various cults, including one dedicated to a god of health and another to the hero Herakles, contributed to his reputation as "loved by the gods" and "the most religious of men." He was celebrated—and worshipped after his death as a hero—for bringing a healing cult (related to Aesculapius and involving a snake) to Athens. It is possible he founded an early version of a hospital. He never flinched from portraying the Greek gods as often wantonly cruel, destroying innocent people, for instance, as punishment for their ancestors' crimes. But the gods in *Antigone*, *Oedipus at Kolonos*, and *Philoktetes* mete out justice with a more even hand.

One remarkable absence in Sophocles' own life was documented suffering of any kind. His luck continued to the moment his body was placed in its tomb. As he lay dying, a Spartan army had once again invaded the Athenian countryside, blocking access to Sophocles' burial site beyond Athens' walls. But after Sophocles' peaceful death the Spartan general allowed the poet's burial party to pass through his lines, apparently out of respect for the god Dionysos.

Robert Bagg

James Scully

NOTE

1. Unless otherwise indicated, the line numbers and note numbers for translations of Sophocles' dramas other than *Elektra* refer to those in the Harper Perennial *Complete Sophocles* series.

Elektra

INTRODUCTION

"HAVEN'T YOU REALIZED
THE DEAD . . . ARE ALIVE?"

awn is breaking. From a hilltop in Mycenae, three men—the Elder, Orestes, and Pylades—look down on a palace haunted by three generations of kin murder. The trio has traveled a distance: for two of them this is a long-delayed homecoming.

The Elder, a trusted, forthright slave, has been a mentor to Orestes, the son of Agamemnon, hero of the Trojan War. Orestes was just a young boy when his father returned from battle. That day, during a celebratory feast, Agamemnon's wife, Klytemnestra, and her lover, Aegisthus, murdered Agamemnon, splitting his skull with an ax. Orestes' sister Elektra, fearing for her brother's life, entrusted Orestes to the Elder, who spirited him away to a safe exile. He grew up in northern Greece, sheltered by Pylades' family. Elektra has since lived in misery, impatiently awaiting her brother's promised return to avenge their father, while Klytemnestra and Aegisthus, now married, nervously rule Mycenae.

The Elder now impresses on both younger men the magnitude and urgency of the job ahead. He, too, is impatient with his young master. Their plans must be in place before the palace awakes. Prompted to take charge, Orestes calmly lays out a strategy, aware that Klytemnestra and Aegisthus fear he might at any moment descend on them. He instructs the Elder to pose as a messenger with news that Orestes has died in a horrific chariot accident. Then, their victims' vigilance relaxed, Orestes and his accomplice Pylades, also in disguise, will carry out the killing. Despite Orestes' apparent command of the situation, he grows uneasy. Faking his own death could prove a dangerous omen. What if *pretending* he's dead precipitates the real thing? Shaking off the thought, he reveals that his motive is not revenge per se, but taking back the power and wealth Aegisthus and his mother have stolen from him.

For fifth-century Greeks, to "help one's friends and harm one's enemies" was an unquestioned maxim governing personal, political, and international conflicts. But Sophocles suggests— at first almost subliminally via the unattractive nature of his main characters—that cycles of revenge ravage those trapped within them as well as their enemies. By portraying Orestes as icily efficient and materialistic, and his sister Elektra as brave but nearly deranged with hatred for her mother and Aegisthus, Sophocles discourages his audience from accepting the looming act of vengeance as a sacred obligation that will ennoble those who undertake it.

The acrimonious and legalistic debates in the first third of the play, between Klytemnestra and Elektra, reveal the instability of the moral ground each invokes to justify homicide or revenge. Klytemnestra argues that killing Agamemnon was justified. A decade earlier, he had sacrificed their daughter Iphigenia to placate the goddess Artemis and thus gain a favorable wind for the Greek army anxious to sail for Troy. Klytemnestra insists his blood relation to his daughter should have out-weighed his obligation to prosecute a war. Elektra counters by saying that the sacrifice of Iphigenia was not criminal: it was a military necessity. Though both claim to argue from the *talio*, the concept of justice as an "eye for an eye, a life for a life," each manipulates and ignores evidence and principle. Their legalisms cannot disguise the ferocity of their antipathies. Klytemnestra wanted Agamemnon dead so she could marry Aegisthus. Elektra hates her mother for killing the father she mourns. Sophocles makes clear that it's impossible to sanction revenge, a gut issue for those involved, simply through analysis and debate. Revenge, the audience realizes, issues from hatred immune to logic or morality.

When the Elder brings news of Orestes' 'death,' Elektra is devastated and Klytemnestra elated. Orestes and Pylades ratchet up the tension when they arrive with an urn they claim holds Orestes' ashes and ask to present it to the queen. Moved by his sister's despair and ravaged appearance, Orestes tells her, with excruciating deliberation, who he really is. But when her out-of-control joy threatens to alert their intended victims, Orestes tries to silence her. Elektra remains oblivious to danger. As her grip on reality grows increasingly tenuous, she confuses the Elder with her dead father and falls to her knees before him. The Elder, untouched, flares up. It seems Orestes and Elektra are too preoccupied with their reunion to realize they have to kill Klytemnestra before her husband and his men return. The Elder must keep them focused on the business at hand. For a moment, it seems doubtful the conspirators fully grasp the seriousness of what they're doing.

Athenian audiences in the last half of the fifth century BCE were familiar with previous dramatic versions of Orestes and Elektra, especially Aeschylus' *Oresteia* trilogy. Sophocles, departing from Aeschylus' version of the myth, allows Elektra's obsession with revenge to absorb and dissolve all other energies and desires. She is disturbed and disturbing. The Chorus of townswomen is by turns supportive and disapproving of her conduct, but to Elektra their sentiments are irrelevant. For her, revenge is an entrenched imperative, and she fully accepts that it has unbalanced her: "[H]ow could I be calm / and rational? Or god-fearing? / Sisters . . . I'm so immersed / in all this evil, how / could I *not* be evil too?" (343–347).

Sophocles' most imaginative departure from Aeschylus involves the seeming omission of the Furies, the ancient, ugly, and relentless divinities who haunt and punish kin murderers. In Aeschylus' version, they are grotesquely real, a terrifying swarm who appear as the eponymous chorus of his play *The Eumenides* (literally and ironically, "The Kindly Ones"). Aeschylus' Furies chase Orestes across Greece until Athena domesticates them by granting them a less violent but more acceptable role. Although Aeschylus shows Orestes suffering the guilt that the Furies inflict on him, he's eventually cleansed of pollution in Delphi and spared civil punishment by the Areopagus court. Sophocles, however, saw that while priests and jurors may absolve a murderer of public guilt, they cannot undo the mental damage that killing a relative inflicts on the killer.

R. P. Winnington-Ingram proposed that Sophocles intended his audience to perceive Elektra and Orestes—throughout the entire length of the action—as *proxy* Furies who pursue and take revenge on Klytemnestra and Aegisthus (1980, 236–247).

By taking this revenge, the siblings become first "agents" and then ultimately "victims" of the Furies now embedded in themselves. They suffer a warping of their decency as they pursue a vengeance that in time will be visited on *them* when a new generation of avengers seeks them or their children out.

At various moments Orestes elaborates on his foreboding that using his faked death as a ploy to exact revenge will backfire—or, in Winnington-Ingram's terms, that his role as an agent of revenge will make him its victim: first, he identifies with a soldier, mistakenly reported dead, who returns home alive to find himself revered; later, Elektra cherishes what she thinks are her brother's ashes and he savors the effect of his death on others; and finally, Aegisthus realizes Orestes did not die in a chariot wreck, but is alive and about to kill him, a living metaphor of how those murdered emerge from death to exact vengeance.

Aegisthus flinches as he uncovers Klytemnestra's body.

Orestes   Scare you? An unfamiliar face?

Aegisthus These men! *Have got me*—I've stumbled
into a net with no exit. Who *are* they?

Orestes   Haven't you realized by now "the dead"—
as you perversely called them—*are alive*? (1787–1791)

The last scene evokes an image of Orestes (and Elektra as well) as victims of the revenge just taken:

Aegisthus . . . why force me inside? If what
you plan is just, why do it in the dark?
What stops you killing me right here?

Orestes   Don't give *me* orders. We're going where
                    you killed my father! You'll die there!
Aegisthus Must this house witness all the murders
                    our family's suffered—and those still to come?
Orestes   This house will witness yours.
                    That much I can predict.
Aegisthus Your father lacked the foresight you boast of.
[. . .]
Orestes   Justice dealt by the sword
                    will keep evil in check.   (1812–1821, 1831–1832)

Orestes might have the last word, but Aegisthus' ominous prediction conveys an unwelcome truth: when it comes to Greek blood feuds, only the extinction of each and every antagonist ends them. Orestes believes killing Aegisthus and his mother will punish and discourage evil, but Aegisthus' assertion—that Orestes and Elektra will remain subject to an implacable curse on the house of Atreus—reasserts the self-perpetuating nature of revenge. Newer Furies, Aegisthus is confident, will sooner or later attack and destroy his killers. The abrupt end of the play, which gives no sense of elation at the mission accomplished shared by the conspirators, leaves the audience to ponder what indeed do this brother and sister have to celebrate?

Elektra

CHARACTERS

ELDER, long-serving slave, teacher, and adviser to
    Orestes

ORESTES, son of Agamemnon and Klytemnestra

Pylades, noble companion of Orestes

ELEKTRA, daughter of Agamemnon and
    Klytemnestra, ragged, unkempt, and bruised

CHORUS of Mycenaean women

LEADER of the Chorus

CHRYSÒTHEMIS, daughter of Agamemnon and
    Klytemnestra

KLYTEMNESTRA, widow of Agamemnon, wife
    of Aegisthus, co-murderer of Agamemnon

Maidservant to Klytemnestra

Aide to Orestes, male

AEGISTHUS, husband of Klytemnestra, co-killer of
    Agamemnon

*The ELDER, ORESTES, and Pylades appear on a backstage hilltop, looking
out over the heads of the audience at the cityscape beyond. As the ELDER
recognizes familiar landmarks, he directs ORESTES' attention to them.*

ELDER

And now, son of the man who commanded
our armies at Troy! Son of Agamemnon!
Look! You can see with your own eyes
the sight you have craved for so long:
the storied Argos of your dreams.
Hallowed country, over which
the horsefly hounded Io, that daughter
of Înachos Hera made a cow.
Look *there*, Orestes. The outdoor market
named after Wolfkiller Apollo.   10
On the left is that famous temple of Hera's.
Believe it. What you see is Mycenae!
Gold city, with its house of Pelops
bloodied by all that death and mayhem.
Under orders from your sister,
I carried you away, even
as your father was being murdered.
I saved your life! Raised you to take
revenge—the strapping youth who gives
his dead father his honor back!   20
All right, Orestes—you too, Pylades,
our excellent new friend—our plan
of attack must be worked out quickly.
Nothing's left of the starry night.
Already you can hear the birds
singing up the dawn, loud and clear.
Before anyone leaves that house,
get it together. The moment's arrived.
No time to dither. Time to act.

ORESTES

                            My best friend,
my mentor! You've always come through   30
for our family! Like an old thoroughbred
who doesn't spook in a tight spot
you stick your ears out straight,
urging us on, charging
into the thick of it. You're
always right there beside us.
Here's what I think. Listen
closely. If anything I say
is off target, correct my aim.
I went to Delphi to ask Apollo—   40
through his Pythian oracle—
how best to avenge my father.
Kill his killers.

                    Apollo said: ALONE NO TROOPS
NO ARMOR BY STEALTH SLAUGHTER
WITH YOUR OWN RIGHTEOUS HAND.
That's what the god told me.

(to the ELDER)

So you must infiltrate the palace.
Seize the first chance you're given.
Find out what's going on, so you
can bring us hard information.   50
You're so old now. After all these years
they won't know you, they won't
suspect you, not with that gray hair.
Now here's your story. You're a stranger
from Phokis. Phantíus sent you.

He's their most powerful ally.
Tell them—and flesh it out—the good
news that Orestes had the horrible
luck to be killed in a chariot race.
He was thrown from his racing car   60
at the Pythian games in Delphi.
Make that the gist of your account.
Meantime we will honor Father
exactly as the god told us to do.
We'll pour milk mixed with honey
over his grave. Next we'll shear off
and leave him thick hanks of our hair.
Then we'll come back here, bearing
a bronze urn into the palace.
We've stashed it in the underbrush,   70
but I think you knew that.
We're sure to pick up their spirits
with the false news that this living
body of mine has been consumed
by fire. Now it's . . . nothing but ashes.

ORESTES *pauses, takes in the ominous implication of his own words.*

Why should this omen bother me—
by feigning my death I take back
my life! I make my name. I don't
think unlucky words can curse you—
if they work to your advantage.   80
Haven't I seen smart men
rumor themselves dead—

so when they do come home alive
the awe they inspire lasts a lifetime?
I'm counting on this bogus tale
to do the same for me. I'll rise
from death, flush with life—flaming
like a starburst over my enemies!

*ORESTES and his companions descend from their hilltop; as they do,
the palace walls light up in the dawn. ORESTES turns from the
now-looming palace to face the city, the surrounding countryside,
and the audience. Over a small rise on stage right is a path leading
to the nearby tomb of Agamemnon. Outside the palace is a statue
of Apollo and smaller statues of the house of Pelops' domestic deities.
The palace façade has an oversize double door. A smaller entrance is
on the far stage left.*

Land of my fathers! My people's gods! Welcome
me! And let my mission succeed.   90
And you, vast rooms my fathers built,
the gods have brought me home
to give you a righteous cleansing. Don't
drive me disgraced from my homeland.
Return our family's house to me.
Let me take power and rule what's mine.
Enough talk. Now it's up to you,
Graybeard. You do your job
and we'll do ours. Now *is* the time.
In whatever men do, timing's the key.   100

ELEKTRA

(within, in a low but resonant voice)

O what a rotten life!

ELDER

A servant? Behind that door.
Commiserating with herself.

ORESTES

Could that be Elektra? Shouldn't we wait?
Hear why she moans?

ELDER

(forcefully)

                        NO! Before anything else
we must obey Apollo. Begin
those libations for your father.
They'll bring victory within reach.
Make sure we control the situation.

*The ELDER exits stage left toward the palace's side entrance; ORESTES
and Pylades move to the right, toward Agamemnon's nearby tomb. Enter
ELEKTRA from the house gates.*

ELEKTRA

(singing)

Pure Sunlight! Air breathing   110
over the whole Earth!
How often have you heard
as darkness dies into day

me singing my sorrows,
pounding fists on my breasts
until blood breaks the skin?
And you, my rancid bed in that
palace of pain, you've heard
me, awake until dawn, crooning
mournful songs for my father, whom   120
Ares the bloodthirsty war god
never welcomed—when he fought
barbarians—to a brave death
and a hero's grave. So my mother
and her bedmate, Aegisthus,
laid open his skull like loggers
splitting oak with an ax.
No anguish broke from anyone's
lips but mine, Father, at your
repulsive, pitiful slaughter.   130
I won't stop mourning you—
not so long as I see stars
brilliant in the night sky,
not while I can see, still,
day breaking over the land.
I'm like the nightingale
who killed her children,
crying to everyone, outside
what used to be my father's door.
Hades! Persephone! Hermes!   140
And *you*, lethal Curses
I scream out loud!
You Curses who can kill!

And you Furies—
you daughters of Zeus,
who strike when you see
an innocent life taken,
or a cunning wife leading
a lover to her bed—
Furies, help me avenge   150
my father's death!
Give me back my brother!
I lack the strength to keep my grief
from dragging me under. I need help.

Enter CHORUS *of Mycenaean women from stage left, walking in small groups from town center. The following lines through line 250 are sung or acted as a duet.*

LEADER
Elektra, why do you
go on like this? *Why*, child?
Yes, your mother's atrocious. But
your grief never lets up—it goes
on and on, bemoaning Agamemnon.
It's been such a long time   160
since your ungodly mother
connived with that evil
bastard to cut him down.
May his killer be killed—
if I'm allowed such a prayer.

ELEKTRA

You're such considerate caring
women—coming here to coax me
out of my misery.
I know your concern, I feel it,
I'm not unaware—but   170
I can't let go, I can't
quit doing this until I'm done.
I can't stop mourning
my murdered father.

              Friends,
you're always gracious, no matter
what mood I'm in. This time
let me be. Let me rage.

LEADER

Grief and prayer
can't bring your father
back from the swamp of Hades.   180
Someday we'll all sink into it.
But you're grieving yourself to death.
Yours is a grief that can't be quenched.
How will you ever satisfy it?
It will kill you! Tell me, *why
do you* love misery so much?

ELEKTRA

Only a callous child forgets
a parent who died horribly.

I'm like the nightingale, forever
mourning its child—*Littlewheel!*   190
Littlewheel!—that grief-crazed bird
Zeus sends to tell us it's spring.
And you too, Niobe, to me
you're the goddess of sorrow
in your tomb, tears running
forever down your stone face.

LEADER

You're not the only one who grieves . . . you just
take it much harder than your sisters inside,
Chrysòthemis and Iphianassa. They
go on living . . . as your young brother does.   200
He's restless in seclusion, ready
for Zeus to start him trekking—
proud of his heritage, awaiting the day
Mycenae welcomes Orestes home!

ELEKTRA

I'm waiting for him too.
I haven't given up,
getting through day after
daylong day, wishing he'd come,
doing all the chores a childless
unwed woman does, always   210
teary-eyed, hemmed in by my own
doom feeling, which never lets up.
My brother's forgotten everything.

All he went through, all he witnessed.
Has he sent me one message
that hasn't proven false?
Always aching to join me—but
for all the aching, never acts.

LEADER

Courage, child, and don't lose hope.
Zeus still watches us from the skies,   220
his power is huge—he controls
all that we do down here.
Let him handle your bitter quarrel.
Be vigilant—your foes hate you—
but don't let your own hatred
get ahead of itself. Time is a god
who eases us through the rough patches.
And Agamemnon's son, grazing
his oxen, is far from indifferent.
And nothing ever gets by   230
the god who rules Acheron
in the world under our own.

ELEKTRA

Hopeless frustration
devoured my youth.
My strength's gone. I dry up
in childless solitude
with no lover to protect me.
Like an immigrant

everyone scorns,
I slave in my father's house,   240
wear rags, eat on my feet.

LEADER

On the day he came home
we heard a heartbreaking
scream—when your father lay feasting
and the bronze blade arced
a quick unswerving blow.
Guile set it up, but lust
did the killing:
a monster was born
from that monstrous coupling—   250
whether humans were
behind it, or a god.

ELEKTRA

It was a day more acrid
than any in my life.
And that night! The terrors
of that unspeakable banquet—
the hacking, no mercy shown
by the slashing hands of that pair.
The same treacherous hands that took
me prisoner and fed me death.   260
May great Zeus on Olympus
punish them, may their glitter
give them no pleasure—
after what they did.

LEADER

You'd better stop talking.
Don't you see? How you stir
up trouble for yourself? Your spirit's
forever on the brink of war.
Don't force it. Don't provoke
fights you can't win.   270

ELEKTRA

I'm forced to be outrageous
by the outrage all around me!
I *know* how passionate I am.
How could I not know?
But what drives me
is so extreme . . .
I can't stop, not while I still
live and breathe. Let it go. Let me be!
Who in her right mind, dearhearts,
thinks *words* could console me?   280
There is no cure. I'll never quit
grieving, or stifle what I sing.

LEADER

But can't I *speak* as though I care,
like a mother! One you can trust?
Who tells you to stop reliving
old grievances time after time?

ELEKTRA

How do you measure misery?

Tell me this: how can it be right
for us to abandon our dead?
Is anyone ever born that cold-blooded?   290
I'll never go along with that—
and never, even if lucky enough
to live once more in comfort,
never would I cling to self-
centered ease, or dishonor
my father by clipping
the wings of my shrill grief.
If we let the dead rot in dirt   *not being accorded*
and disregard, while those killers   *honor by society*
pay none of their own blood   300
for the blood of their victims, all
respect for human beings, all respect
for law, will vanish from this Earth.

LEADER

I'm here for your sake, daughter,
but also for my own. If what
I'm saying doesn't help, go your
own way. We're with you still.

ELEKTRA

Sister, I'm ashamed if you think
I grieve too often and too much.
But the compulsion is so strong—   310
I must. So forgive me.
What woman from a great family

could hold back, watching her father's
house suffer disaster? It's still
happening! All day, all night long.
It never withers, but blooms and blooms!

It begins with the mother
who bore me and hates me.
I live by the sufferance
of father's murderers.   320
They say if I eat. Or don't.
Think what my days are like.
Aegisthus sits, propped up
on father's throne in the great hall
—wearing my father's clothes—
pouring libations on the same
hearthstone where he killed him.
Worse than that, the killer
sleeps in my father's bed
with my mother, if that's   330
the right word. Mother? *Slut!*
So shameless she lives with,
lays herself under, that
piece of pollution. She's not
intimidated by the Furies—
she mocks her own depravity.
Now, waiting an eternity
for Orestes to come end this,
inside me I'm dying.
He's always *going* to do it   340

but never does—it's taken
all the hope out of me.
So how could I be calm
and rational? Or god-fearing?
Sisters . . . I'm so immersed
in all this evil, how
could I *not* be evil too?

LEADER

What about Aegisthus? Suppose
he hears you talking like this?
Or has he gone somewhere?   350

ELEKTRA

Of course he's gone.
If he were anywhere near here,
you think I could stroll out the door?
He's off in the fields someplace.

LEADER

If that's true, can we talk freely?

ELEKTRA

He's not around! Ask your question.
What's your pleasure?

LEADER

What about your brother?
You think he'll come? Or keep
putting it off? I'd like to know.   360

ELEKTRA

Says he'll come. Never does what he says.

LEADER

When a man's about to take on
something overwhelming—
won't he sometimes hold off a bit?

ELEKTRA

(coldly furious)

When I saved *him*, did I "hold off a bit"?

LEADER

Easy now. He's a good man.
He won't let his own people down.

ELEKTRA

Oh I trust him. I'd be
already dead if I didn't.

LEADER

(whispering)

Shhh! Don't talk.   370
I see Chrysòthemis—your real sister,
the one you share both parents with—
coming out of the house carrying
food and drink to offer the dead.

Enter CHRYSÒTHEMIS from the palace.

CHRYSÒTHEMIS

Making more trouble, sister?
Come out of the house on the street side,
have you, so you can rant in public?
What about?
Haven't you learned yet not
to indulge in pointless fury?   380
Listen, I too hate the way
we're made to live.
Had I the power, I'd let them know
I don't love them either. But
in waters rough as these
I'm going to reef sail,
not make threats, when I can't
possibly do them any harm.
I'd advise you to do the same.
Of course your rage is justified.   390
You do speak for justice. I don't.
But if I want to live my life freely,
I've got to do everything our rulers
tell me to do. No exceptions.

ironic
not free if
your rulers
dictate what
you do

ELEKTRA

Strange, isn't it? That the daughter
of such a father should dishonor him
to humor a mother like ours.
She's taught you how to bawl me out.
Not one syllable is your own!
It's your choice: either act bravely—   400

or play it safe and betray
those you should love the most.
Weren't you just now telling me, *if*
you only had the power, you'd hate
them for the whole world to see!
Yet now when I'm doing all I can
to avenge Father, you back down.
You try to make *me* back down.
On top of everything . . . cowardice.
Tell me—no, let me tell *you*—what   410
do I gain if I stop grieving?
Now, I'm *alive*. Miserable,
for sure, but it's enough for me.
I give *them* grief—and that comforts our dead,
if they can feel pleasure in Hades.
But you, bragging about your hatred?
Your hate is *spoken*. When it comes to action,
you're in the camp of Father's killers.
I'll never surrender to them,
even if they tried to bribe me   420
with privileges they buy you with.
Keep your seat at their rich table.
Eat your fill. Enjoy your luxuries.
For me it's sustenance enough
that I don't starve my conscience.
I don't hunger for what you've got.
Nor would you, if you knew better.
But now, when you could be called
child of the best father ever, you

choose to be your mother's daughter.   430
People will call you a traitor to your
dead father and those who love him!

LEADER

No more angry talk! Please!
Elektra, Chrysòthemis, can't you
learn something from each other?

CHRYSÒTHEMIS

Learn what? I've heard all this before.
My friends, I wouldn't bring
this matter up, but I've heard
something truly evil will cut short
her incessant lamentations.

ELEKTRA

What kind of "evil"? Let's hear it!   440
If it *is* worse than my life now,
I *will* shut up for good.

CHRYSÒTHEMIS

All right, I'll tell you what I know.
They're going to shut you up
in a cave, in another country.
You won't see any sun down there,
but you can still feel sorry for yourself.
Face that prospect. Think about it.
Don't blame me when it's way too late.

ELEKTRA

That's what they plan to do to me?   450

CHRYSÒTHEMIS

Yes. When Aegisthus gets back.

ELEKTRA

That's it? Then I hope he comes soon.

CHRYSÒTHEMIS

You're crazy! What a sick wish!

ELEKTRA

Let him come, if that's what he intends.

CHRYSÒTHEMIS

So you can suffer? How insane is that?

ELEKTRA

It will put plenty of distance
between me and the likes of you.

CHRYSÒTHEMIS

You've no interest in the life you still have?

ELEKTRA

Oh what a lovely life I have.

CHRYSÒTHEMIS

It could improve. If you'd restrain yourself.   460

ELEKTRA

Don't give *me* any lessons in betrayal.

CHRYSÒTHEMIS

I don't teach that. Just . . . give in to power.

ELEKTRA

Give in to *them*? That's your way, not mine.

CHRYSÒTHEMIS

Better than suicidal folly.

ELEKTRA

If I'm killed, I'll do it fighting for my father.

CHRYSÒTHEMIS

I know Father forgives what I'm doing.

ELEKTRA

Cowards comfort themselves with pieties like that.

CHRYSÒTHEMIS

So you won't wake up? And take my advice?

ELEKTRA

Forget it. Be a while before I'm that desperate.

CHRYSÒTHEMIS

OK. I'll go finish my errand.   470

ELEKTRA

Go where? Who are those offerings for?

CHRYSÒTHEMIS

They're from our mother. For Father.

ELEKTRA

What are you saying? For her worst enemy?

CHRYSÒTHEMIS

                                        "The man
she killed with her own hands"—as you'd put it.

ELEKTRA

Who put her up to this? Who wanted it done?

CHRYSÒTHEMIS

She was reacting, I think, to a nightmare.

ELEKTRA

Oh you family gods! At last you're with me!

CHRYSÒTHEMIS

What terrifies her, inspires you?

ELEKTRA

First tell me her dream. Then I'll explain.

CHRYSÒTHEMIS

I know very little of it.   480

ELEKTRA

Then let's hear that. One little word
has often made men or broken them.

CHRYSÒTHEMIS

Word has it she saw our father in sunlight,
come back to sleep with her again.
He took hold of the scepter—his own, once,
though now Aegisthus carries it around—
and planted it by his hearth. Instantly
a fruit-laden bough shot up from it,
casting darkness all over Mycenae.
I heard this from someone who was there—
when she was telling her dream to the Sungod.   490
That's all I know—except . . . because of that
alarming dream, she sent me on this errand.

ELEKTRA

Don't, my dear sister, do this.
Don't let any of these offerings
touch his tomb. They're from a wife he hates!
Neither custom nor devotion allows food
or drink to be passed on to our father from *her*.

No. Let the wind blow them away.
Or bury them deep, at a distance.
Leave Father's tomb undisturbed. Then,   500
when she's dead, *she* can dig them up.
If she weren't the most unfeeling of women,
she'd never try to pour remorse
offerings over the grave mound
of the husband she murdered.

Think now. Is it likely he'd take
these honors kindly—from the same hands
that hacked off his extremities?
As if he were an enemy soldier?
Then wiped the blood off on his hair?   510
How could she think what's in your hands
would absolve her of that murder?
It can't. Just throw these things away.
Take him some of your own hair instead,
then something from me—though I'm such a mess.
I've nothing to offer but my unwashed hair.
And this sash—no baubles stitched into *it*.

*ELEKTRA unties her plain cloth belt and, using the knife hanging from it, cuts
off a lock of her hair and hands both to CHRYSÒTHEMIS.*

Then fall face down and pray for him
to rise up from Hades and help us
attack his enemies. Pray that his son   520
Orestes lives—powerful enough to crush
Father's enemies underfoot. So ever after

we may decorate Father's tomb with hands
richer than ours are now. I'm thinking that . . .
Father had something to do . . . with sending
her these terrifying dreams. Go, sister,
honor him. You will do yourself some good—and me—
and him, the most belovèd man ever,
who lives now with Hades. Your father. Mine.

LEADER

Devout advice you'd be wise to take, friend.   530

CHRYSÒTHEMIS

I agree. And I'm duty bound.
There's no reason to weigh
any alternatives.
I'll do it now. And while
I do it, tell no one.
If mother hears what I'm up to,
I think I'll regret it.

CHRYSÒTHEMIS exits.

CHORUS

(singing)

If I'm not some deluded prophet,
Justice, who sent us this signal,
will strike the righteous blow   540
herself, and strike soon, child.
I'm breathing in the sweetness
of that reassuring dream.

The lord of Hellas, who
begot you, hasn't forgotten.
That keen, bronze, twin-bladed ax
hasn't forgotten either—forced to strike
the savage blow that killed him.
The Fury whose legs never tire,
who waits in her deadly ambush,   550
will destroy with an army's might
the wicked—still blazing with the lust
that flung them on a stolen bed, then
into a guilt-cursed, blood-drenched
adulterous marriage.
We'll see, I don't doubt,
this nightmare omen
punish the criminal pair.
And if it fails to happen
we mortals are hopeless   560
at reading the future
from oracles or dreams.
Curse the chariot race
Pelops ran generations ago!
It doomed your family forever,
scattered disaster in its wake—
when dazed Myrtilos sank
to his rest on the sea bottom
after a murdering hand shoved him
deathward off that golden racing car.   570
Since then, this house has never
been free from savagery and grief.

Enter KLYTEMNESTRA.

KLYTEMNESTRA

I see you're running around loose—
because my husband isn't here
to stop you sneaking out the gates—
where you embarrass the family.
And with him gone you couldn't care
less about me. Forever telling people
I'm a tyrannical bitch who puts
down you and all you care about.   580
But don't charge *me* with insolence.
You lash out at me, I lash back!
Your father—now *this* always sets
you off—was killed by me. True.
I'm sure he was. Without a doubt.
But it was Justice herself, *not
just me*, who killed him. And Justice
is a goddess you should respect,
if you had any sense whatever,
knowing that this father of yours,   590
the one you can't stop crying over,
was the only Greek generous
enough to please the gods by killing
his own daughter—he, who never felt
what a mother feels giving birth.
So tell me this: why, or to please
whom, did he sacrifice her life?
Dare you say: to please the Argives?

No. They had no right to kill her.
Or if he was obliging his brother   600
Menelaus when he killed my daughter,
shouldn't he owe me his death—for that!
Menelaus had two children, *they*
should have been sacrificed before
my child was—*their* parents caused that war!
Or did Hades have some perverse
craving to feast on *my* children,
not Helen's? Or had this heartless father
stopped loving children born from my womb,
loving instead those from that whore?   610
What sort of sick, selfish parent
would do that? Oh, you disagree?
But wouldn't your dead sister
side with me, *if* she had a voice?
I regret nothing I have done,
and if you think I'm cold-blooded,
ask how impartial your judgment is
before you condemn someone else's.

ELEKTRA

You can't say, this time, that something
I did provoked what you've just said.   620
But if you'll permit me, I'll tell you
the truth about my father and sister.

KLYTEMNESTRA

Go ahead. Permission granted.

If you always spoke in a tone
this calm, it wouldn't be so painful.

ELEKTRA
All right, I'll talk to you. You said you killed
my father. Could you say anything
more damning? Whether you killed him
justly or not? But killing him
wasn't just. No. You were seduced   630
to murder him by the criminal
lowlife who is now your husband.
Ask Artemis, who looks after hunters,
what crime she punished when she stilled
the sea breeze at Aulis to a dead calm.
No! Let *me* tell you. She never would.
Here's what I know. My father once
was tracking game, when his footsteps
startled a stag with a giant rack.
He shot it down, recklessly   640
whooping a boast about his kill.
Outraged, Artemis then becalmed
the Greek fleet, demanding *this*
price for killing her forest creature:
that he sacrifice *his own daughter*!
That's how it happened. How she died.
Otherwise the fleet was marooned.
Couldn't sail to Troy *or* sail home.
That was Father's predicament—he
was forced to make the choice he did.   650

He was bitterly reluctant,
but he did finally kill her.
And not for Menelaus' sake!
But let's suppose you're right. That he
did do it to help out his brother.
Would that justify killing him?
With your own hands? What law was that?
Take care. If you invent a law
and apply it to all humankind, won't it
inflict guilt and grief back on you?   660
For if it's going to be blood for blood,
you'll be the next to die,
you'll get the justice you deserve.
Take a hard look at your own life.
Living openly with a killer
who helped you slaughter my father?
You started a family with *him*—
cutting off your legitimate children
who have done nothing wrong. You have!
Who could approve the things you've done?   670
You married Aegisthus to avenge your
daughter? What a coarse claim: marry
an enemy for your daughter's sake?
Why am I even giving you advice?
You shout that I disparage my mother.
Well, I think you're much less
a mother than my slavemistress,
so rotten is the life I lead,
kicked around by you and your mate.

Then there's the one who got away,   680
who slipped through your fingers, pathetic
Orestes, bored stiff, rotting in exile.
You accuse me of raising him
to make you both pay for your crimes;
I would have done that—if I could.
You better believe it. Go ahead,
tell everyone I'm treacherous
if you like. Tell them I'm strident,
that I'm brazen—because if I
possessed all those traits   690
I'd be a daughter worthy of you.

LEADER

(to KLYTEMNESTRA)

Lady, I can tell you're seething.
But ask yourself. Could she be right?

KLYTEMNESTRA

(to CHORUS)

Should I care how I treat her—a grown
woman abusing her mother! Is there
one thing she'd be ashamed to do?

ELEKTRA

I'll tell you one! I *am* ashamed
of my rage, though you won't see why.
I know my conduct's unbecoming

for a woman my age.   700
It's utterly unlike who I was.
But your hostility, your actions—
they have made me do things
that aren't in my nature.   *out of touch w/ true*
I'm so given to disgusting   *self*
displays because they're all around me.

KLYTEMNESTRA

Aren't you a piece of work. Obsessed
with *Who I am, what I say, what I do*!
I give that mouth of yours
way too much grist to grind.   710

ELEKTRA

You said it! I didn't! Right.
What you *do* provokes what I *say*.

KLYTEMNESTRA

Artemis will make you
pay for your insolence
when Aegithus gets back.

ELEKTRA

Look at yourself—fuming mad,
out of control! You want me
to speak—then you don't listen.

KLYTEMNESTRA

Then won't you just shut up
and allow me to sacrifice?
Now that you've had your say?   720

ELEKTRA

Go ahead, sacrifice.
I won't get in your way.

KLYTEMNESTRA

(to a Maidservant carrying a basket)
Girl! You. Lift those fruits up high,
so I may start praying to our god.
And quiet the anxiety I feel.

KLYTEMNESTRA looks up at the statue of Apollo.

You have protected us a long time,
Apollo, my lord. Do listen
attentively to me now. My language
may be somewhat oblique, because
I'm not among friends here.   730
It wouldn't be wise to speak
plainly, since she can hear.
Her loud spiteful mouth will spew out
exaggerated versions all over town.
No, listen the same way I speak:
aware of what I'm implying.

Promise me, Wolfkiller, if signs I saw
in my perplexing dreams last night

seem harmless, make sure they come true.
But if they seem to you dangerous,   740
turn them against those who hate me!
If anyone plots to throw me
out of this house, and steal my wealth,
stop them! Allow me to go on
living in the house of Atreus,
ruling this kingdom, enjoying
the company of those living with me now.
Spare the offspring who don't hate me.
Lose those who blame their pain on me.
Hear me, Wolfkiller Apollo.   750
Grant me all that I pray for.
Other matters that concern me,
must, since you are a god,
be on your mind, even if I
don't mention them at all.
Surely a son of Zeus
sees everything there is.

The ELDER enters from stage left where he has quietly waited.

ELDER

Ladies, please help a stranger
who'd like to know if this palace
belongs to your ruler, Aegisthus.   760

KLYTEMNESTRA

It does, stranger. You've guessed right.

ELDER

And I imagine this lady is . . .
his wife? She looks like a queen.

LEADER

That she does. You're in the presence.

ELDER

Greetings, my lady. I have sweet news
for you and Aegisthus. From a friend.

KLYTEMNESTRA

I'll take that as a good omen.
But first, tell me who sent you.

ELDER

Phantíus the Phokaian.
On a vital matter.   770

KLYTEMNESTRA

How vital, sir? Let's hear it. Since
it comes from a man we admire
I'm sure we'll like his news.

ELDER

Orestes is dead. That's my news.

ELEKTRA

I'm devastated. Today I die!

KLYTEMNESTRA

What, stranger? What!!
Don't listen to that one.

ELDER

I'll repeat what I said. Your son's dead.

ELEKTRA

Then I am. I don't exist.

KLYTEMNESTRA

(to ELEKTRA)

Then go bury yourself! Stranger,   780
tell me exactly how he died.

ELDER

That's why I'm here. To tell it all.
Orestes had just come into the stadium—
intent on competing in the most high-stakes
athletic games in Greece, those at Delphi—
when he heard a man bellowing
that the sprint was about to start.
It's always the games' first event.
So Orestes steps to the starting line
on fire, impressing the onlookers.   790
He led the pack from start to finish,
walking off with the laurel crown.
I'll skip most of it, there's so much
to tell: nobody matched this man

in what he did and what he won.
In each event the marshals staged
he took the laurels every time—
sprints, middle distances, pentathlon.
People assumed he had uncanny luck.
Time after time the herald boomed out: 800
"Orestes the Argive, born
to Agamemnon, who marshaled
once the armed might of Greece!"
So far, so good. But when a god
takes you down, not even a great
strong man escapes. There came the day
for chariots to race at dawn.
He joined a crack field of drivers.
First on the track was an Achaean,
then a Spartan. Two expert drivers   810
up from Libya. Next Orestes
with mares from Thessaly,
the fifth team to join the parade.
The sixth entry, an Aetolian,
drove chestnut colts. A Magnesian
was seventh, and eighth to appear
came four white Aenian stallions.
The ninth team was from the godbuilt
city, Athens, and one last entry,
the tenth, was out of Boeotia.   820

All teams were settled into lanes
the race stewards had drawn by lot,

the trumpet blared, and they took off,
urging their horses on, shaking
their reins in their fists, the stadium
resounding with chariot racket,
each trailing a plume of dust, cutting
each other off in mass confusion,
slashing their horses' backs without
mercy, each driver determined   830
to overtake the wheels, the snorting
horses of his competitors—
wet gusts of the horses' foaming breath
drenching their backs and churning wheels.
Orestes cut the pillars close
at both ends of the race course—
as his wheels grazed by the posts
he slackened the outside horse's reins,
pulling back hard on the inside left-
hand horse. Till now all chariots   840
had managed to avoid over-
turning, but the Aenian's stiff-
mouthed three-year-olds bolted sideways,
swerving into the seventh team's path,
butting heads with the Barkarian's
stallions. Other sideswipes followed,
smashup on smashup, crash after
crash, clotting the entire track
with tangled wreckage of race cars.
Reacting quickly, the skittish   850
Athenian pulled his horses off

to one side and slowed, allowing
the surge of chariots to pass him.
Orestes too laid off the pace,
in last place, trusting his stretch run.
But when he saw the Athenian,
his only rival, still upright, he whistled
shrilly in the ears of his fast fillies
to give chase. The teams drew even,
first one man's head edging in front,   860
then the other's, as they raced on.
Till now Orestes had gone clean
through every circuit of the track,
rock solid in his well-built car,
but then, as he loosened the right rein
going into a turn, his left wheel
caught the post, breaking the axle
box open, throwing him over
the chariot rail, snared in the reins,
smashing the ground as his mares spooked   870
across the infield of the racetrack.
When the crowd saw that he'd been thrown
it gasped in pity for the brave lad
so suddenly, hideously doomed,
gouging earth, feet kicking at sky,
till the other charioteers,
fighting their runaway horses
to a standstill, cut him loose, so
soaked in blood no friend who knew him
whole would know his disfigured corpse.   880

They burned him on a pyre right there,
right then. Picked men from Phokis
are transporting what's left of him
in a small urn—the sorry dust
and ashes of that mighty
physique. So that his home country
can see to his worthy burial.

CHORUS

(with emotional murmuring)
Our ancient rulers are wiped out—
their roots, their limbs, wiped out.

KLYTEMNESTRA

O Zeus! What has happened?   890
Can I say—it's good news?
Or horrible—yet a blessing?
It's so harsh—that a calamity
makes my life safe.

ELDER

Why does my news depress you, woman?

KLYTEMNESTRA

It is so very strange, birthing a child.
Even when a child betrays you,
you can't make yourself hate him.

ELDER

Then it seems I've come here for nothing.

KLYTEMNESTRA

Not for nothing. How can you say that   900
when you've brought proof he's dead—
the boy who got his life from my
life, sucked my milk, yet he deserted me,
went into exile! He's a stranger now.
Having left his homeland, he never
saw me again, but kept on blaming me
for killing his father. He swore
he'd do something terrible to me.
Those threats keep me awake, night
and day. Sleep never shuts my eyes.   1000
I've been forced to live out my life
thinking any moment I could die.
But now it's gone, my fear of him,
and of this girl who's worse—living
inside my house, leeching my lifeblood.
Now that her threats are dead, I'm at peace.

ELEKTRA

Yes, I'm finished. But free to grieve
the crash that killed you, Brother,
while your mother condemns you.
Orestes—aren't I better off?   1010

KLYTEMNESTRA

No, you're not. Yet. He's better off.

ELEKTRA

Listen, Nemesis! How she respects the dead!

KLYTEMNESTRA

Nemesis heard both of us out!
She came to the right conclusion.

ELEKTRA

Go ahead, sneer. Your great moment.

KLYTEMNESTRA

Won't you and Orestes shut me up?

ELEKTRA

We're the ones shut up! How can we silence *you*?

KLYTEMNESTRA

(turning to ELDER)
We'd owe you a great deal, my man,
if you've finally put a stop
to that jarring clamor of hers.   1020

ELDER

Then may I leave? If all is well?

KLYTEMNESTRA

Certainly not! We haven't shown
proper appreciation, to either you
or to our good friend who sent you.
Come inside. We'll leave her out here
crying for herself and her dear departed.

KLYTEMNESTRA and the ELDER enter the palace.

ELEKTRA

What do you think of that? What a mother!
Heartbroken, grief-stricken—an
awesome display of maternal
feeling for a son's ghastly death.
She tosses off a snide slur   1030
as she takes her leave. Makes me sick.
Orestes, your death kills me too.
You've stolen my last hope—
that you'd come back, avenge
your father and what's left of me.
Now I have nobody. I'm alone.
As bereft of you as of Father.
I'll go back to being enslaved
by people I despise. His murderers.
Aren't things fine with me now?   1040
(stares at the great doors to the palace)
I won't cross that threshold ever—
to live with them. I'll rough it here
next to the gate. A dried-up crone,

I'll have no friends. I won't care
how I look. And if those
inside don't like it, they can do me
a favor and kill me. Life now
will be torture. I don't want it.

LEADER

Why no lightning from Zeus?
Where is the Sun, if he can look at *this*—   1050
and pretend it's not happening?

ELEKTRA

(whispering, then quietly sobbing)
Yes! Where are *They*? Where?

LEADER

Daughter? Why the tears?

ELEKTRA

(now raises her hands at the heavens and screams)
Curse you!

LEADER

Don't scream at *Them*!

ELEKTRA

You'll kill me.

LEADER

For doing what?

ELEKTRA

If you tell me to keep on
hoping the dead in Hades
can still help me, you'll crush
me further—when I'm   1060
already heartbroken.

LEADER

I was thinking of Amphiaraos—whose wife,
bribed with a golden necklace,
convinced him to start the war
that got him killed—yet now
in the world below . . .

ELEKTRA

No! Don't do this.

LEADER

. . . he still lords it there,
his mind robust as ever.

ELEKTRA

(lifting her fists and glaring again at the skies)
Aaagggh!   1070

LEADER

(also looking at the sky)

Aaagggh indeed. For that murderess—at least they killed . . .

ELEKTRA

. . . the killer!

LEADER

Her. Yes.

ELEKTRA

I know! I know that! Those bereaved
people had an avenger!
But who will my avenger be?
The only one I ever had
is dead, and lost to me.

LEADER

You. Your life. Defenseless.

ELEKTRA

I know that. Only too well.   1080
Month after month my life's
a raging flood that keeps
churning up horror after horror.

LEADER

We watched while it happened.

ELEKTRA

Then stop trying to distract me,
when I . . .

LEADER

When you what?

ELEKTRA

. . . no longer have the slightest hope
my royal brother can save me.

LEADER

Everyone alive has a death date.   1090

ELEKTRA

To die like my doomed brother? Tangled in leather,
dragged under the bone-crushing hooves of horses?

LEADER

So cruel it's beyond comprehension.

ELEKTRA

Beyond mine. So far from
my loving hands I couldn't . . .

LEADER

But who could?

ELEKTRA

. . . ready his body for the fire,
bury him, cry over him.

Enter CHRYSÒTHEMIS, out of breath, from Agamemnon's tomb.

CHRYSÒTHEMIS

I'm so elated, sister—my feet flew—   1100
it isn't ladylike, I know,
to race here so fast. But I've got
great news. Your past troubles,
your grieving? Over. Done with!

ELEKTRA

How could *you* have found a cure
for *my* suffering? I can't imagine.

CHRYSÒTHEMIS

(still speaking in bursts)
Orestes! *Here.* He's alive.
As I am. Here. *Now!*

ELEKTRA

Are you out of your mind, girl?
Making fun of my pain? *And* yours?   1110

CHRYSÒTHEMIS

I swear by our father's hearthstone.
I'm not joking. I'm telling you he's *here.*

ELEKTRA

Oh my. You innocent. Where did you
get such a story? You believed it?

CHRYSÒTHEMIS

I believe it because my eyes saw it!
I didn't *get it* from anyone.

ELEKTRA

You're so naïve! Where's your proof?
What did you *see* that has you red-faced,
as if you'd caught some deadly fever?

CHRYSÒTHEMIS

For god's sake, listen, please.   1120
Hear me out. Then decide
how "naïve" I am, or not.

ELEKTRA

Go ahead. Talk. If it makes you happy.

CHRYSÒTHEMIS

All right, I'll tell you everything I saw.
As I walked toward Father's ancient
grave site, on top of the mound I saw
fresh milk running down it, his urn
decorated with all kinds of blossoms.
I was stunned. I looked to see
if anybody was around anywhere,   1130

but no. It was very quiet.

I got closer to the tomb. So help me,

there, on its edge, was a swatch of hair.

That instant my breath caught,

I flashed on the face I most loved—

I knew it was his hair,

a signal from Orestes that he's back!

I cupped it in my hands, careful

not to say anything unlucky.

Right away my joystruck eyes   1140

teared up. I'm sure now, just as I

was then: that hair was *his* hair.

Who else would have, could have

left it? Except us. It wasn't me.

How could it be you? You can't leave

the house, not even for prayers,

without great risk. As for Mother,

she wouldn't do such a thing.

She *couldn't* have done it. We'd've known.

No, the hair left in tribute at the tomb   1150

could only be Orestes' doing.

Look up, sister, show some spirit!

Nobody's luck is always rotten.

Ours was horrific once. Maybe today

will show us it's getting better,

ELEKTRA

While you spoke, all I could

feel was pity for you.

CHRYSÒTHEMIS

What's wrong? Why didn't my news thrill you?

ELEKTRA

You've wandered clear out of this world.

CHRYSÒTHEMIS

How could I mistake what I just saw?

ELEKTRA

Our brother's dead. There's no chance
he'll come save us. Don't hope he will.   1160

CHRYSÒTHEMIS

Ohhh! Whoever told you that?

ELEKTRA

The man who saw him die.

CHRYSÒTHEMIS

Where is this person? My mind's reeling.

ELEKTRA

Inside. Mother's giving him a warm welcome.

CHRYSOTHEMIS

Then who put all those tributes on the tomb?

ELEKTRA

Someone who wanted to honor
Orestes, now that he's dead.

CHRYSÒTHEMIS

Stupid! Here I'm rushing
to you with good news—
ignorant of the mess we're in.   1170
Now that I'm here, I find
worse grief waiting to crush me.

ELEKTRA

So you have. But trust me.
You can lift this weight off.

CHRYSÒTHEMIS

By raising the dead back to life?

ELEKTRA

I didn't mean that. I'm not a fool.

CHRYSÒTHEMIS

What would you have me do?
Something I really *can* do?

ELEKTRA

Yes. If you've got the nerve to join me.

CHRYSÒTHEMIS

If it will help us, how can I refuse?   1180

ELEKTRA

Anything worthwhile . . . has risks.

CHRYSÒTHEMIS

I'm with you, as far as I can be.

ELEKTRA

Then listen. Here's my plan. Nobody
here will help us. You must know that.
We're alone. Our men are in Hades.
I had hoped, while my brother lived,
he'd come back to avenge his father.
Now that he's dead, I'm turning to
you—to help me kill father's killer.
Aegisthus. I won't keep   1190
anything from you. From now on.
How long are you willing to wait
doing nothing? Who else will do it?
Sure you can bitch you've been robbed
of Father's wealth—that you're too old
now for a wedding, for married love.
So don't keep hoping you'll enjoy
its benefits. Aegisthus isn't
so thickheaded he'd let us have
sons who would be sure to kill him.   1200
But if you act on my plan, our dead
father in Hades will approve,

so will our brother. What's more,
you'll be a free woman, you'll make
a good marriage, for true courage
is something everyone values.
And as for men talking about us,
don't you see the fame we'll win
if you will just listen to me?
Can you imagine any citizen,   1210
any *stranger*, who wouldn't be
impressed? "Look at those two sisters,
they saved their father's house—
brought down their dug-in enemies,
without a thought for their own lives!"
That's what they'll say about us.
Dead or alive, we'll be famous.
Do it, sister. Work with your father,
help your brother and me, free us all
from any further suffering.   1220
A shameful life shames anyone
born to a family as noble as ours.

LEADER

In situations like this,
foresight's a friend, of both
speaker and spoken to.

CHRYSÒTHEMIS

(to CHORUS)
Right, and before she said a word,
women, if she had any sense,

she'd have remembered plots like hers
often go wrong. But she forgot about that.

(to ELEKTRA)

What are you trying to accomplish,   1230
making recklessness your weapon,
and calling on me to do the same?
Don't you get it? You're a woman,
not a man. You don't have
the strength our enemies command.
Their power grows, ours wastes away.
Who could plot to kill such a man
without being themselves cut down?
You'll make the trouble we're in worse
should anybody overhear us.   1240
If we win fame then get killed, what
possible good does that do us?
I'm begging you, before we die,
forever wiping out our family,
control yourself. I guarantee
no one will know what you just said,
nobody's going to get hurt.
You should learn to respect power
when you have none of it yourself.

LEADER

(sharply, to ELEKTRA)

Listen to her. Nothing's more vital   1250
than thinking clearly—and thinking ahead.

ELEKTRA

(to CHRYSÒTHEMIS)

You're so predictable. I knew
you'd hate what I have in mind.
I'll act alone. I'm not quitting.

CHRYSÒTHEMIS

Too late! I wish you'd shown
this much spunk the day Father died.
Then you could have brought it all off.

ELEKTRA

I had the impulse, not the brains.

CHRYSÒTHEMIS

Then work on that.   1260

ELEKTRA

Is that why you won't help me *do* something—
because you think that *I'm* naïve?

CHRYSÒTHEMIS

You are. Any attempt to kill him will fail.

ELEKTRA

I envy your cool self-control.
I hate your spinelessness.

CHRYSÒTHEMIS

I'll listen as coolly to your
praise as I do to your insults.

ELEKTRA

Don't worry. You'll hear no praise from me.

CHRYSÒTHEMIS

The future lasts a long time. It will decide.

ELEKTRA

Go away. You're no help at all.   1270

CHRYSÒTHEMIS

I could help. You're incapable
of understanding how I could.

ELEKTRA

Go. Tell all this to your mother.

CHRYSÒTHEMIS

No. I may hate you. But not like that.

ELEKTRA

Then admit your lack of respect!

CHRYSÒTHEMIS

Lack of respect? I am
trying to save your life.

ELEKTRA

Do you expect me to follow
your idea of what's just?

CHRYSÒTHEMIS

Yes! When you get your sanity back,   1280
then you might show us the way.

ELEKTRA

It's depressing when someone so
well-spoken can go so wildly wrong.

CHRYSÒTHEMIS

That's a perfect description of you.

ELEKTRA

How so? You think I'm being *unjust*?

CHRYSÒTHEMIS

Justice itself can sometimes wreak havoc.

Justice maybe isn't worth it if it creates chaos in society

ELEKTRA

I'm not willing to live by laws like that.

CHRYSÒTHEMIS

If you're dead set on doing this, you'll
end up admitting I was right.

ELEKTRA

My mind's made up. You don't scare me.   1290

CHRYSÒTHEMIS

Better think it through one more time.

ELEKTRA

There's nothing more to think about.

CHRYSÒTHEMIS

You haven't understood a thing I've said.

ELEKTRA

I worked this out long ago. Not just now.

CHRYSÒTHEMIS

Well, if you call that sense,
keep on thinking like that.
When you find out how much trouble
you're in, you'll think better of what I said.

Exit CHRYSÒTHEMIS abruptly into the palace.

CHORUS

(singing)
When we see airborne birds
instinctively cherish the parents   1300
who fed them and raised them,
why don't we ask why

we don't treasure *our* parents,
our children, the same way?
When the lightning of Zeus
strikes targets chosen by Themis,
the goddess of Justice,
agony's on them in an instant.
You voices of the dead
who burrow under the earth,   1310
carry your heart-wrenching summons
to Agamemnon in Hades.
Tell him that he's dishonored here,
that discord ravages his house,
that sisters, battling each other,
tear asunder the caring web
of their life together,

how Elektra, abandoned,
braves fierce seas of sorrow
mourning her father's doom   1320
tirelessly, like a nightingale
scornful of death, prepared
to leave sunlight forever
if she could purge the twin
Furies—like the loyal daughter
she is—from her father's palace.
No decent person
prefers to live a life
of squalor, blacken
her decency, amass   1330

a legacy of shame.
So you, my girl,
make grief a weapon!
You scorn disgrace,
fighting for, and winning,
two kinds of glory,
for wisdom, and for being
the best daughter alive.

In power and wealth may you
tower over your enemies   1340
as they now lord it over you.
Fate has beaten you down,
that I see. Yet here you are
winning fame where it counts,
driven by the great laws of our nature,
inspired by your reverence for Zeus.

Enter ORESTES *and Pylades stage right with an Aide carrying a bronze urn.*

ORESTES

Ladies—the directions we were given—
have they brought us to the right place?

LEADER

What place? What are you looking for?

ORESTES

I'm looking for where Aegisthus lives.   1350

LEADER

Well whoever told you to come here
told you right. That's his house.

ORESTES

They've been expecting us. For some time.
Will someone tell those inside we've arrived?

LEADER

(indicating ELEKTRA)

This young woman. *If* it's right
for close kin to announce you.

ORESTES

Go right in, girl, tell them men
from Phokis are looking for Aegisthus.

ELEKTRA

(reacting to the urn the Aide carries)

No! No! You're not bringing us proof
the rumor that we've heard is true?   1360

ORESTES

I know nothing of any rumor.
Old Strophios sent me with news of Orestes.

ELEKTRA

What news? I'm afraid what I'll hear!

ORESTES

(gestures to the urn carried by his Aide)

He's dead. Look how small an urn he's in.
There wasn't much left to bring home.

ELEKTRA

(crying gently)

I'm heartsick to see, at last, my misery.
Which you hold there in your hands.

ORESTES

If you weep for Orestes' suffering—
what there is of him is right here.   1370

ELEKTRA

Let me hold it in my hands, sir, please.
If this urn really holds him, I'll weep
and keen for myself, our whole family.
Not only for these few ashes.

ORESTES

(to his Aide)

Come over here. Give it to her,
whoever she may be.
If she wants it that badly.
She's not someone who hated him
but a friend, most likely blood kin.

ELEKTRA

(taking and holding the urn)

Dearest remains of you I loved   1380
best on Earth, Orestes, nothing
is left of you but *this*. So different
from what I hoped you'd become
when I sent you away. And this
is how you come home. My own hands
lift you like you're nothing. Yet how
radiant was the boy I sent off!
I should have died before these hands
picked you up and packed you off
to a strange land, to keep you   1390
from being murdered. Better
you were killed the same day
your father was, and buried beside him.
Now, remote from your homeland
and your sister, you've died a grim death.
My grieving hands didn't, as was my duty,
wash and dress your body, or scrape
the sad remnant from the ravenous fire.
No. Hands of strangers did this
for you, long gone brother, and now   1400
as ashes in an urn they bring you home.

My loving care, my bathing you
so long ago—seems a waste now.
You were never your mother's child,
you were mine! No one in our house

nursed you but me, the one you called sister.
Now in one day that's gone—
like a whirlwind you've sucked up
everything, taken it with you.
Father's gone. You've killed me.   1410
Our enemies gloat. That unmothering
mother is mad with joy, the one
so many times in secret letters
you promised me you'd punish.
But your bad luck and mine
has sent you home to me
as this!

ELEKTRA sifts the ashes through her fingers.

        Not the shape
of one I loved. The ashes of a ghost.

Dear lifeless dust!
When you raced on that terrible circuit,   1420
dear brother, see how you've killed me.
I was wrecked by your side. Now,
take me with you. To your new home.
I'll join my nothingness to yours.
We'll be there forever, together, below.
Up here, we share even our doom.
I'd like to die now. Don't leave me
behind. The dead, I can see, feel no pain.

LEADER

Elektra! Think! Your father was mortal.
So was your brother. You shouldn't   1430
grieve too much. We're all going to die.

ORESTES

(breathes in and out a huge sigh)
What should I say?
When the right words won't come?
I can't use my own tongue.

ELEKTRA

What's wrong with you? Why did you say that?

ORESTES

Are you the famous Elektra? *The* Elektra?

ELEKTRA

I am myself. In the pit of misery.

ORESTES

I'm sorry, truly, for this horrible misfortune.

ELEKTRA

Surely, stranger, you can't be sorrowing for me.

ORESTES

Someone was abused. Atrociously.   1440

ELEKTRA

Nobody fits your grim words like me. Stranger.

ORESTES

What kind of life is this?
Ummarried. Despondent.

ELEKTRA

Why are you staring at me like that?
Why this concern at what you see?

ORESTES

I didn't know I had so much to grieve for.

ELEKTRA

What's been said to make that apparent?

ORESTES

I *see* your miseries. They ravage you.

ELEKTRA

You see very little of my misery.

ORESTES

What could be worse, that I don't see?   1450

ELEKTRA

I live in the same house with murderers.

ORESTES

Whose murderers? What are you getting at?

ELEKTRA

My father's. They made me their slave. By force.

ORESTES

Who forces you to be a slave?

ELEKTRA

She's called my mother. Doesn't act like one.

ORESTES

How so? She beats you? Demeans you?

ELEKTRA

Beats, starves, demeans, everything.

ORESTES

No one has ever come to help you? Or stop her?

ELEKTRA

One would have. You gave me his ashes.

ORESTES

Poor woman. I've pitied you a long while.   1460

ELEKTRA

You are one of a kind. No one else has.

ORESTES

The only one who's come. Who shares your pain.

ELEKTRA

You aren't some distant relative?

ORESTES

I'd answer that, if I could trust these ladies.

ELEKTRA

They're friends. You words are safe with them.

ORESTES

Give me the urn. I'll tell you everything.

ELEKTRA

Don't ask me to do that! For gods' sake!

ORESTES

Do as I say. You won't ever go wrong.

ELEKTRA

(clinging to the urn and gripping ORESTES' chin with her free hand)

Do you love this? Then don't steal him I love!

ORESTES

(placing a hand on the urn)

You can't keep this.   1470

ELEKTRA

(speaking to the urn)

If I can't bury you, Orestes,
I'll be devastated.

ORESTES

Don't talk like that. You tempt fate!
You have no right to grieve.

ELEKTRA

(outraged)

No right to grieve for my own brother?

ORESTES

It's not a good thing for you to mourn him.

ELEKTRA

My dead brother thinks I'm not good enough!

ORESTES

(his hand is still on the urn)

He feels no disrespect for you. This isn't yours.

ELEKTRA

It is, if these are his ashes.

ORESTES

They're not. That's just a story.   1480

ORESTES gently takes the urn from ELEKTRA and hands it to his Aide.

ELEKTRA

Then where *is* my dead brother buried?

ORESTES

Nowhere. The living don't inhabit tombs.

ELEKTRA

Young man, what are you saying?

ORESTES

Nothing . . . that isn't true.

ELEKTRA

He's alive?

ORESTES

If I am. Alive.

ELEKTRA

He . . . is *you*?

ORESTES

(removes and hands ELEKTRA his signet ring)
Look at this signet. Our father's.
Tell me if I speak true.

ELEKTRA

O day . . . of light!   1490

ORESTES

Mine too.

ELEKTRA

Your voice! It's you. You're here!

ORESTES

I'll never be anywhere else.

ELEKTRA throws her arms around ORESTES, embracing him for a while, then stands close to him, looking into his eyes until he turns away at line 1538.

ELEKTRA

It's you I'm clinging to.

ORESTES

Don't ever not . . . hold me.

ELEKTRA

(turning to address CHORUS)
Dearest friends, dear citizens,
look! It's Orestes! Who deceived us
into thinking him dead, yet by that
deception, he lives again!

LEADER

We see him, daughter.   1500
After so much has happened to you both
your happiness has us crying with joy.

ELEKTRA

Son of the father I loved,
you're here at last! Come
to find those you love!

ORESTES

I'm here. But say nothing. Yet.

ELEKTRA

Why not?

ORESTES

We'd better keep it quiet.
Someone inside might hear us.

ELEKTRA

Artemis knows, eternal virgin that she is,
those housebound women don't scare me.   1510
They're worthless—dead weight on the Earth.

ORESTES

Women are warlike too.
I believe you've experienced that.

ELEKTRA

Yes I have. And you bring me back
to a bitterness nothing can hide.
One I can't outlive or forget.

ORESTES

That I know just as well as you.
So when the trouble starts
remember all they did.

ELEKTRA

Every moment of the future,   1520
as we live it, will be the right
moment for my fury—only
now are my lips free to speak.

ORESTES

So they are. Keep them free.

ELEKTRA

How? What should I do now?

ORESTES

Don't talk too much. It's not the time.

ELEKTRA

But how could I by *silence*—show
how glad I am you're back?
I never hoped, never believed
I'd see your face again.   1530

ORESTES

You see my face . . . because . . .
the gods inspired me to come.

ELEKTRA

Then it's a greater miracle
than if you'd come on your own—
a god sent you! It had to be:
the gods are in on this.

ORESTES

I'm reluctant to curb your joy,
but it's so *intense* it scares me.

ORESTES, agitated, turns away from ELEKTRA, who loses her grip on him.

ELEKTRA

After all these years, after
coming here, meaning   1540
everything to me . . .
Oh don't, not *now*, seeing me
in all my misery . . .

ORESTES

(turning back toward ELEKTRA)
Don't what?

ELEKTRA

(reaching to take his face in her hands)

Don't take away the joy I feel
just looking at your face.

ORESTES

I would be angry . . . if
someone else tried to stop you.

ELEKTRA

Then you agree?

ORESTES

How could I not?   1550

ELEKTRA

Brother, your voice was one
I never thought I'd hear again.
I suppressed what I felt,
kept quiet, didn't shout
when I first heard its sound.
Now that I'm holding you,
I see your face light up, the face
that in the depths of my grief
I could never forget.

ORESTES

(abruptly, refocused on his task)
Let go of it. No excess words.   1560
Don't explain how evil
our mother is, or how Aegisthus

siphons off Father's wealth,
wasting it on pointless
opulence—don't, because
you won't know when to stop.
Just tell me what I need to know *now*—
when the coast will be clear
or where we can ambush
our enemies—so our   1570
arrival freezes their laughter.
Make sure your mother doesn't
guess your intentions.
Don't let your face glow
when you enter the palace.
Stick to your grief,
pretend my false death
really happened.
When we're victorious,
then we can laugh, breathe   1580
easy, and celebrate freely.

ELEKTRA
Brother, what pleases you pleases me.
You brought me joy when I had none.
And I'll accept nothing for myself,
no matter how much it might mean,
if it would inconvenience you.
Doing so would put me in the way
of the god who's befriending us.
You know how things stand here.

Aegisthus is somewhere outside.   1590
Mother's inside. But don't worry.
She'll never see my face light up.
My hatred for her runs too deep.
Since you've come home, I feel
so much joy it makes me cry.
How could I not? One moment
you're dead, the next, you're not!
You've made me believe *anything*
can happen. If Father reappeared
alive I wouldn't think I'd gone   1600
crazy, I'd believe what I saw.
Now you've come so amazingly back
home, tell me what you'd have me do.
If you'd never come, one of two
things would have happened. I'd have
killed my way to freedom, or died trying.

ORESTES

Quiet! I hear someone coming out.

ELEKTRA

Go inside, friends. No one will stand
in your way—considering what you carry—
though there's no joy in it for them.   1610

Enter the ELDER, furious, through the great doors.

ELDER

Fools! Are you children bored with life?
Born with no sense in your head?
Can't you see? You're not *near* danger,
you're *in* it. If I hadn't watched
at the door, word of your plans would
have wafted in ahead of your bodies.
I've taken care to spare you that.
But now stop jabbering, stop
your giddy racket. Get in there!
Hanging back *now* means disaster.   1620
Come on, get on with it.

ORESTES

What are my chances in there?

ELDER

Excellent. No one will know you.

ORESTES

You *have* reported my death, right?

ELDER

To them, you're a shade among shadows.

ORESTES

Are they in high spirits? What are they saying?

ELDER

Save that for later. When we're done.
As things now stand, everything's fine.
Even things that might not seem fine at all.

ELEKTRA

Who is this person? For gods' sake, tell me!   1630

ORESTES

You don't see?

ELEKTRA

See? What.

ORESTES

You don't recognize the man
whose hands you gave me to?

ELEKTRA

Man? What man?

ORESTES

The man who took me to Phokis,
thanks to your own quick thinking.

ELEKTRA

One of the few we could trust,
after Father was murdered?

ORESTES

Yes! Stop questioning me!   1640

ELEKTRA

(kneeling at the ELDER's feet)

Dear light! You, you alone
saved Agamemnon's house.
How did you get here? Are you *really*
the one who saved my brother and me
from unending sorrow?

ELEKTRA seizes the ELDER's hands.

Dear hands! Dear faithful servant
whose feet so kindly walked you here,
how *could you* be near me so long—
unrecognized? You gave no hint
who you were. I didn't know you!   1650
You misled me with fictions—yet
they held a sweet reality.
O blessings, Father—for in you
I see my father! Know that in one day
I've hated and loved you more
than any man in the world.

ELDER

(abruptly, yet kindly)

That's enough! As for the story
of what went on while I was gone,

our days and nights to come
will make all of it clear.   1660
(turning to ORESTES and Pylades)
But I'm telling you two, *still*
standing here, you *must act*. Now.
Klytemnestra's alone. No men
are inside. But, if you hang back,
think how many you'll have to fight—
not just servants, but trained killers.

ORESTES

He's right, Pylades, no more talk.
Let's go—once we've paid our respects
to my father's gods on our porch.

ORESTES, Pylades, and the ELDER pause to pray briefly to Apollo's statue,
then enter the palace. ELEKTRA addresses the statue and kneels.

ELEKTRA

Apollo, lord, please honor their prayers   1670
and mine, too. Often I have come
to offer you what little I possessed.
But now, Wolfkiller Apollo, I come
with all I have, on my knees. Help us.
I beg you. Take an active part
in our plans. Show how gods
break those who break your laws.

ELEKTRA enters the palace.

CHORUS

(singing)

See how Ares comes on:
his breath . . . breathing . . . bloody
vengeance no one outruns.
Already into the rooms, his   1680
relentless hounds tracking evil—
what my soul dreamed
soon will be done.

He who stands up for the dead
moves soundless through
the power and wealth
of his father's ancient home—
the edge of his vengeance
newly honed ahead of him,
while Hermes, Maia's son, keeps   1690
his guile dark, till the finish line's
crossed, and all delay dies.

ELEKTRA comes out of the palace but pauses in the doorway to look back at what's happening inside.

ELEKTRA

Dear women, the men are
about to finish it.
Yet wait. Be quiet.

LEADER

Finish it? What do you mean?

ELEKTRA

She's getting the urn ready
for burial. They stand next to her.

LEADER

Then why are you out here?

ELEKTRA

I'm watching for Aegisthus.   1700

KLYTEMNESTRA sends a bloodcurdling shriek from deep in the house.

KLYTEMNESTRA

(screaming within)
NOOOOO! No guards!
Assassins in the house!

ELEKTRA

Someone's screaming in there! Hear it?

LEADER

I can't bear to! I'm still shaking.

KLYTEMNESTRA

(from within)
Aaaagggh! Aegisthus!! *Where are you Where are you?*

ELEKTRA

Again! Someone screaming.

KLYTEMNESTRA

(from within)

My child, my own son, pity your mother!

ELEKTRA

(shouting back)

You had none for him! *Or* his father!

LEADER

Doomed kingdom. Doomed family.

The destiny that shadowed you   1710

day after day is done now.

KLYTEMNESTRA

(from within)

My god I'm stabbed!

ELEKTRA

(shouting)

Stab her again—

if you have the strength.

KLYTEMNESTRA

(from within)

*Aaaaah*gain!

ELEKTRA

I wish it struck Aegisthus too.

CHORUS
(singing)
The Curses work!
The buried live!
Blood for blood flows
from veins opened   1720
by those murdered
so long ago.
          And here they are!—

—enter ORESTES and Pylades, bloody—

hands smeared with blood
sacrificed to the war god.
I can find nothing to blame
in what they've done.

ELEKTRA

Orestes . . . how did it go?

ORESTES

It went well. If
Apollo oracled well.

ELEKTRA

Is that wretch dead?

ORESTES

                      Nothing to fear.   1730
She'll never demean you again.

LEADER

(looking offstage right)
Quiet! Here's Aegisthus.

ELEKTRA

Boys, back inside!

ORESTES

Which way is he coming?

ELEKTRA

From the fields. Smiling. He's ours.

LEADER

(to Pylades and ORESTES)
Go in! Quick! Wait in the entryway.
You've done the first job well,
but there's one more to do.

ORESTES

Don't worry, we'll do it.

ELEKTRA

Hurry! Get going.   1740

ORESTES

We're gone.

ELEKTRA

I'll see to things here.

ORESTES and Pylades go inside.

LEADER

(to ELEKTRA)

Speak gently to him. So he'll walk

blind into combat with Justice.

Enter AEGISTHUS.

AEGISTHUS

Who can tell me where those Phokaians are—

I hear they're telling us Orestes

was killed in a chariot wreck.

(addressing ELEKTRA)

You! Yes you! You're always outspoken.

I think you've a lot at stake here.   1750

You must know what's happened. Tell me.

ELEKTRA

Of course I know. If I didn't,
I'd be ignorant of what's
befallen my nearest kinfolk.

AEGISTHUS

Then tell me where the strangers are.

ELEKTRA

Inside. They've found a way
into the heart of their hostess.

AEGISTHUS

Did they really report him dead?

ELEKTRA

Even better. They've shown us a body.

AEGISTHUS

I'd like to see this corpse with my own eyes.

ELEKTRA

You can, but it won't be an agreeable sight.

AEGISTHUS

But you've just given me agreeable   1760
news. And that's not like you at all.

ELEKTRA

If you can take pleasure in it,
go ahead, celebrate.

AEGISTHUS

(shouting as if to servants inside the palace)
Enough. Open the doors, let all
Mycenaeans—and all Argives—
observe. Whoever put hopes in this man,
seeing his body, will now take my bit
in his mouth, willingly—without
waiting for my lash to break his spirit.

ELEKTRA

(starts swinging the heavy doors open; ORESTES and Pylades help from
inside)
Oh I've learned *my* lesson. Time has taught   1770
me to join forces with those stronger than me.

The doors open fully, revealing a covered bier with ORESTES and Pylades
standing beside it.

AEGISTHUS

O Zeus. Only avenging gods
could permit this unpleasant sight.
But if I have offended Nemesis,
whose reprisals are always just,
I'll take back what I've just said.

Uncover his face. Since he was
blood kin, I should mourn him.

ORESTES

Lift it yourself. It's not for me
to do, it's for you—to look at   1780
these remains, and speak well of them.

AEGISTHUS

You're right. Of course. Good advice, well taken.
(to ELEKTRA)
Will you call Klytemnestra? If she's near?

ORESTES

She's close by. No need to look far.

AEGISTHUS lifts the cloth.

AEGISTHUS

My god. What *is* this?

AEGISTHUS flinches as he reveals KLYTEMNESTRA's body.

ORESTES

Scare you? An unfamiliar face?

AEGISTHUS

These men! *Have got me*—I've stumbled
into a net with no way out. Who *are* they?

ORESTES

Haven't you realized by now "the dead"—   1790
as you perversely called them—*are alive*?

AEGISTHUS

(pauses a beat)
Oh yes. That's a puzzle I've solved.
This must be Orestes I'm talking to.

ORESTES

How come, though you're a discerning
prophet, we deceived you so long?

AEGISTHUS

We're done. Ruined. But
give me just one brief word . . .

ELEKTRA

For gods' sake, brother,
don't let him talk!
You'll get a *speech*!   1800
He's going to die.
What good does it do
to drag this out?
Kill him now. Throw his corpse
somewhere way out of sight—
scavengers will give him
the burial he deserves.
Nothing else will free me
from all I've been through.

ORESTES

(to AEGISTHUS)

Get inside! Now! Move! This isn't   1810
a debate, it's an execution.

AEGISTHUS

Then why force me inside? If what
you plan is just, why do it in the dark?
What stops you killing me right here?

ORESTES

Don't give *me* orders. We're going where
you killed my father! You'll die there!

AEGISTHUS

Must this house witness all the murders
our family's suffered—and those still to come?

ORESTES

This house will witness yours.
That much I can predict.   1820

AEGISTHUS

Your father lacked the foresight you boast of.

ORESTES

More words. You're stalling. Go.

AEGISTHUS

After you.

ORESTES

Go in first.

AEGISTHUS

Afraid I'll escape?

ORESTES

(to AEGISTHUS in a calm, confiding tone)
No. To keep you from dying
where you choose. I want your death
to be bitter and without mercy.
Justice should always be instant—
for anyone who breaks the law.   1830
Justice dealt by the sword
will keep evil in check.

Other forms of punishment?

CHORUS

(facing the palace façade)
House of Atreus, you've survived
so much grief, but what's been
accomplished today sets you free.

ALL leave, except ELEKTRA, who remains, standing alone, until the lights dim or the curtain falls.

NOTES TO THE PLAY

6–13 *Hallowed country . . . house of Pelops* The Elder serves here not only to pinpoint the sights for Orestes and Pylades, but also to evoke the legendary and horrific legacy of the house of Pelops and Atreus.

7 *horsefly hounded Io* Zeus seduced Io, whereupon Zeus' wife Hera turned her into a cow and arranged to have her chased over the countryside by a giant buzzing horsefly.

9 *outdoor market* The market square, dedicated to Apollo, and Hera's temple were the city's most famous landmarks, though the temple would not be visible from the actual heights where the trio pauses.

13 *Pelops* The house of Pelops, whose name was given to the entire region still known as the Peloponnesus, began with Pelops' father Tantalos, who offered his son to Zeus and the god's divine cohorts as the entrée at a banquet brazenly intended to test the gods' powers of perception. Zeus, not fooled or pleased, restored Pelops to life. Pelops fathered Atreus, who became king of Mycenae, and eventually adopted his grandsons, Agamemnon and Menelaus. Through further episodes of cannibalism, incest, adultery, and kin murder, this dynastic family continued to foster the hatred and treachery we see as the play opens.

21 *Pylades* The son of Strophios, king of Phokis, and Anaxibia, the sister of Agamemnon, with whom Orestes lived while growing to manhood and preparing to return to Argos and avenge his father.

29–30 *My best friend . . . mentor* The initial role of the "Pae-dogogus," as he is named in the Greek manuscripts, was to oversee Orestes' education, but he has assumed the duties of a friend and adviser as Orestes reached maturity.

40 *I went to Delphi* Orestes had determined to kill Klytem-nestra and Aegisthus before consulting the sibyl at Delphi; he did not ask Apollo whether to do so was advisable. He simply asked how best to carry out the murders. Apollo sup-plied a plan and made no effort to discourage him.

76 *Why should this omen bother me* Ambiguous words or physical signs that suggested worst-case scenarios frequently spooked the superstitious Greeks. Here Orestes briefly fears that his feigned death might invite his actual death. He reas-sures himself by remembering that famous travelers and war veterans were known to feign death as a ploy to enhance their reputations as survivors.

ORESTES and his companions descend from their hilltop In the original staging, it was likely that the trio appeared atop the roof of the skenê behind the façade of the palace, to rep-resent their excellent vantage. After Orestes completed his long speech, they would have descended and entered the or-chestra from stage right.

122–123 *when he fought / barbarians* Elektra wishes that if Agamemnon was fated to die a violent death, he had died fighting the Trojans (whom she considers barbarians). She regrets that Ares, the war god, deprived her father of such an honorable death.

124–126 *my mother / and . . . Aegisthus, / laid open* Sophocles envisions the murder of Agamemnon as having occurred while he was reclining at dinner on his first night home from Troy and thus unable to see his killers approaching from behind. So positioned, his head would be an easy target for a swung ax.

136 *I'm like the nightingale* Elektra compares herself to Prokne, who killed her own son, Itys, and served him to her husband, Tereus, who had raped her sister Philomela and cut out her tongue to prevent her from exposing him. When vengeful Tereus pursued both sisters, Zeus changed all three to birds, Tereus to a hoopoe, and the two women to a swallow and a nightingale respectively. The resemblance to a bird whose sole powers of complaint are musical suits the fact that the passage in which the metaphor occurs is sung.

140 *Hades! Persephone! Hermes!* All gods of the underworld: respectively, the ruler of the underworld, his semicaptive wife who divides her time each year between the living world and the world of the dead, and the nimble messenger god, one of whose duties is to lead dead souls into Hades' kingdom.

143 *You Curses who can kill!* The Greeks of the Homeric era believed an emphatically uttered curse had the power to kill or damage its target. Note that Elektra takes this verbal power literally though her brother does not.

144 *And you Furies* The (female) Furies were tasked with pursuing murderers of kin until the kin of their victims killed

them or the murderers committed suicide. Though Elektra asks them to intervene, the traditional Furies do not appear in the play. Sophocles, however, suggests at several places that Orestes, Pylades, and Elektra have become human embodiments of Furies and are fulfilling their ancient function in the course of killing Klytemnestra and Aegisthus.

190–193 Littlewheel! . . . *Niobe* Another appropriate mythological counterpart to express Elektra's inconsolable bereavement. Niobe was the daughter of King Tantalos of Lydia. She married Amphion, a king of Thebes, and bore six sons and six daughters to him, according to Homer. She infuriated the goddess Leto by claiming to be a better mother than the goddess, having given birth to twelve children compared to Leto's two. Unfortunately for Niobe, Leto instructed her children (Apollo and Artemis) to murder Niobe's children. Niobe wept for nine days and nights, and the Olympian gods turned her to stone on a cliff of Mount Sipylos, the home of her father, where her rock face continued to drip with tears. "Littlewheel" may refer to Prokne's dead child Itys, whose name in Greek could mean small wheel or circle.

199 *Chrysòthomis and Iphianassa* Elektra's living sisters. Iphianassa does not figure in the play.

231 *Acheron* The river and marsh surrounding the underworld.

364 *hold off a bit* After Agamemnon's murder, Elektra acted swiftly, entrusting the Elder with her brother, Orestes, giving the man instructions to keep the boy safe in another part of Greece, and to train him to return to Mycenae and kill his father's murderers.

444–445 *shut you up / in a cave* A mode of execution that
    avoided the polluting effect on perpetrators who inflicted
    outright kin murder with their own hands or through direct
    orders. See the similar use of death by entombment and star-
    vation in *Antigone*.

476 *reacting, I think, to a nightmare* Dreams and nightmares
    were believed to be sent into sleeping minds by the gods, but
    they needed to be accurately interpreted to illuminate a situ-
    ation or to become prophecies.

508 *hacked off his extremities* This phrase translates the
    Greek verb *emascalisthe* (which also appears in two pas-
    sages from Aeschylus) and refers to the practice of murder-
    ers who would cut off the arms and legs and then tie them
    around the necks of their victims. Though the English
    word "emasculate" derives from the same root, Sophocles
    did not necessarily mean that Klytemnestra emasculated
    Agamemnon. What she did was terrible enough. The word
    also referred to the military practice of amputating an en-
    emy's arms and/or legs after death to humiliate him in the
    underworld.

539 *Justice* The Chorus refers to Diké, whom they assume sent
    Klytemnestra the dream as a warning that this goddess was
    about to strike a deadlier blow.

563–564 *the chariot race / Pelops ran* A moment of treach-
    ery that began the curse afflicting the House of Pelops. In
    order to win Hippodamia as a bride, Pelops bested her fa-
    ther, Oenomaus, in a chariot race. But Pelops had cheated
    and needed to cover up his malfeasance. He had bribed
    Oenomaus' chariot-mechanic Myrtilos to ensure a wreck

(by removing the chariot's linchpin) that killed his master during the race. Later, Myrtilos and Pelops fell out. While both were aboard an airborne chariot (a gift from Poseidon), Pelops hurled Myrtilos to his death. Dying, Myrtilos cursed Pelops so potently that his malice inflicted grotesque acts of revenge on every subsequent generation of the Pelops clan. This origin myth suggests it is no coincidence that Orestes (i.e., Sophocles) chose a chariot race as the setting for the Elder's false story of Orestes' death. When she heard it, Klytemnestra might have been pleased and reassured by the irony: a curse that began with one chariot race conveniently ends with another.

617–618 *ask how impartial . . . before you condemn* This spirited and savage debate in which Klytemnestra seizes the first rounds is a good example of Athenian legal argumentation. Such confrontations suggest that hostility was a constant of this household's daily life. The two women counter each other's positions, but they remain oblivious to the weakness of their own assumptions and red herrings. To kill one's daughter is horrific from any point of view, and Klytemnestra clearly is right in saying that her husband has committed the serious crime of kin murder. But her suggestion that it would have been more appropriate for one of Menelaus' children to have been sacrificed is irrelevant, since it is from Agamemnon that Artemis seeks redress. Klytemnestra's urging Elektra to evaluate the 'justice' of her own argument before responding is wishful thinking.

630–631 *You were seduced / to murder him* Here Elektra nails what (she thinks) was her mother's true motivation for killing Agamemnon. But her speech veers opportunistically from resentment to resentment in a way that such real-life confrontations usually do. Blundell's exacting analysis of their opposing arguments (*Helping Friends and Harming Enemies*, 157–72) demonstrates that Sophocles was in control and aware himself of his two antagonists' valid points and each one's shortcomings. The dramatic function of this showdown is more to expose a snarl of longstanding hostilities than to ask us to adjudicate the matter.

641 *whooping a boast* An inadvisable provocation, though Artemis' wrath seems out of proportion to the offense.

642–647 *becalmed the Greek fleet . . . Otherwise . . . marooned* Perhaps Artemis raised the stakes for the Greek's getting to Troy to dissuade the Atreus brothers from throwing good men after a bad wife.

658–660 *If you invent a law . . . won't it / inflict guilt . . . back on you?* A valid point, one Klytemnestra brushes off. Her actual rejoinder will be to ignore Elektra and appeal to Apollo to weigh in on her side.

737–739 *Promise me . . . If signs I saw . . . seem harmless* A conventional self-protective formula in situations where one cannot be sure that the dreamer is correctly interpreting the intent of the god who inspired the dream.

748–749 *Spare the offspring . . . Lose those* More obliquity. She implies that Chrysòthemis should be spared but not Elektra or Orestes.

782 *That's why I'm here. To tell it all.* The Elder must have spent his offstage time composing this remarkably detailed speech. The Orestes it imagines is far more impressive than

the Orestes who speaks and acts within the play. Blundell (174) suggests the speech represents Elektra's idealized version of her brother. The speech also contrasts the Orestes of the play with the man he might have become.

835 *Orestes cut the pillars close* The race stewards assigned positions at the start line by drawing lots. Orestes has drawn the inmost position, which, as Kells (144) notes, explains his racing strategy (identical to that Nestor gave his son in the *Iliad*): stay in your lane; if other drivers pass you, they will tire from covering more distance; you'll be able to catch them on the last of the twelve laps. The chariots are racing counterclockwise. Rounding them on the innermost lane requires a 180-degree reversal of direction, hence cornering is a highly dangerous maneuver if the charioteer cuts the posts close in order to catch the leader. The forward momentum of the standing driver will naturally throw him forward in front of the chariot when it loses a wheel and drags an axle.

896 *birthing a child* A line that dramatizes the maternal reflexes Klytemnestra feels and then suppresses. She quickly recovers her animosity toward Orestes. The line also nods in passing to the Greeks' belief the mother-child relation is a sacred one. As shrewdly noted by Kells (138–139), the extreme realism of the Elder's account has a profound effect on Klytemnestra: "she is presented with a picture of Orestes whom she only remembers as a little boy, now grown to manhood, distinguishing himself . . . now behaving as a son *of whom she might be proud*. . . . Only such an account . . . could have moved . . . the mother's heart to that . . . amazing *peripeteia* of emotion 896–898 represents."

1012 *Nemesis!* The goddess of payback. An instance of the
   Greek sense that *all gods* listen to all human speech and
   react to offenses within their spheres of intervention.

1050 *Where is the Sun* One of the Sun's roles was to expose the
   guilty so that Zeus knew where to aim his thunderbolts.

1055 *Don't scream at* Them! The Olympian gods, whom Elek-
   tra accuses of failing to punish the guilty.

1062–1063 *Amphiaraos—whose wife, / bribed with a golden*
   necklace Elektra will react hostilely to this invocation of
   Amphiaraos' fate. He was a seer whose wife contrived to
   get him killed during the attack on Thebes by the armies of
   seven cities, as described in *Antigone.* Polyneikes had given
   Amphiaraos' wife Eriphyle a golden necklace in exchange
   for shaming her husband into joining the ill-fated expedi-
   tion. The gods spared him (as a good man betrayed) death
   by slaughter and instead had him swallowed by the Earth in
   a manner similar to Oedipus' entry into the afterlife. After
   death, Amphiaraos' seer-craft did not desert him; he ended
   up as a ruler of the dead. The implication is that the gods
   and the dead will treat Orestes with similar respect.

1071 *Aaagggh indeed* As Jebb (1894, 121) interprets this cryp-
   tic exchange, Elektra's scream arises from the fact that Am-
   phiaraos' wife was punished for killing him, but her father,
   Agamemnon, remains unavenged. The Leader takes Elek-
   tra's cry to mean, "So much for Eriphyle's treachery," and
   responds, in effect, "Yes, yes!" The chorus starts to say,
   "for the murderess," intending to continue, "who killed her
   husband!" Elektra, however, can think only of the differ-
   ence between the two outcomes, interjecting, "was brought

down." I have adjusted the translation to maintain the rapid-fire quality of the exchange.

1299–1300 *airborne birds / instinctively cherish the parents* The bird referred to here is probably the stork, whose example of parent-child reciprocity was noted by Aristotle *Av.* 1355. (Jebb, *Elektra*, 145)

1306 *Themis* The goddess of justice, religious observance, and right action.

1321 *tirelessly, like a nightingale* The nightingale of the Prokne myth. This species became an apt choice to represent ceaseless mourning because it sings all night long.

1324–1325 *twin / Furies* Aegisthus and Klytemnestra.

Aide carrying . . . urn It may be without a lid, but could contain real ashes to allow the actress to show her tenderness toward Orestes' remains.

1420 *When you raced on that terrible circuit* Many scholars interpret this line to refer to Orestes' outward journey into exile in Attica, only to return as ashes. The lines seem also, perhaps even more appropriately, to refer to his fatal circuit of the racecourse at Delphi.

1432 *What should I say?* Orestes is conflicted here. Should he reveal who he is and thus risk that his reckless sister will give him away? Or should he respond to her by relieving her of her misery?

1629 *Even things that might not seem fine at all* The Elder might mean that Klytemnestra has resumed grieving for Orestes, now that she's holding his ashes, and therefore is distracted and not on her guard. (See Kells, 213.)

kneeling at the ELDER's feet The gesture emphasizes Elektra's delusional confusion of the Elder with her dead father.

1681 *relentless hounds tracking evil* A phrase that fuses Orestes and Pylades with the invisible Furies who inhabit them as they kill Klytemnestra.

1688–1690 *the edge of his vengeance / newly-honed ahead of him, / while Hermes* Hermes, earlier invoked by Elektra, and whose function is to usher the doomed into death, arrives to encourage the pair on their deadly mission.

1710–1711 *The destiny that shadowed you . . . done now* The Chorus believes the curse on the House of Atreus has run its course. Though this chorus is more perceptive than many in Sophocles' plays, the unresolved exchange at play's end suggest they might be mistaken here.

1713–1714 *Stab her again— / if you have the strength* Elektra's great moment. Why she thinks Orestes might be incapable of stabbing Klytemnestra again is puzzling. Perhaps her chilling encouragement is meant to discourage any revulsion or second thoughts on her brother's part.

1717 *The Curses work!* See earlier comment about Curses as viable weapons for line 143.

1728–1729 *It went well. If / Apollo oracled well* The line suggests a certain detachment on Orestes' part. He carried out the killings according to Apollo's instructions. If Apollo supplied them sincerely, then everything did go well. If Apollo's terse words concealed a hidden danger, further trouble may be in the wings. Or Orestes may simply refer here to the unfinished business of killing Aegisthus.

1770–1771 *Time has taught / me to join . . . those stronger than me* Elektra's capacity for irony is fully exercised throughout her exchange with Aegisthus. Here she implies for Aegisthus' benefit that she's yielding to his dominance, but by "those stronger" she clearly means Orestes and Pylades.

1790–1791 *Haven't you realized by now "the dead"* . . . *are alive?* Orestes' taunt ties in with the Chorus's apprehension that Orestes and Pylades pursue Klytemnestra and Aegisthus into the palace as if they were ancient "Furies" and in doing so act on behalf of the "dead" Agamemnon.

1817–1818 *Must this house witness all the murders / our family's suffered—and those still to come?* Aegisthus' response to Orestes' declaration of finality is to predict (twice) that the curse on the House of Atreus has yet to run its course.

1831–1832 *Justice dealt by the sword / will keep evil in check* Orestes implicitly claims that justice, achieved by his punishing the latest kin murderers, will put an end to intrafamilial feuds.

1833–1835 *House of Atreus* . . . *what's been / accomplished today sets you free* The Chorus takes Orestes at his word. Does Sophocles?

WORKS CITED AND CONSULTED

Aeschylus. *The Complete Greek Tragedies*. Trans. Richmond Lattimore, ed. David Grene and Richmond Lattimore. Chicago: University of Chicago Press, 1959.

Aristotle. *Aristotle's Poetics*. Trans. Leon Golden. Tallahassee: Florida State University Press, 1981.

———. *The Art of Rhetoric*. Trans. John Henry Freese. Loeb Classical Library 193. Cambridge, MA: Harvard University Press, 1967.

Berlin, Normand. *The Secret Cause: A Discussion of Tragedy*. Amherst: University of Massachusetts Press, 1981.

Blundell, Mary Whitlock. *Helping Friends and Harming Enemies: A Study in Sophocles and Greek Ethics*. Cambridge: Cambridge University Press, 1989.

Boegehold, Alan L. *When a Gesture Was Expected*. Princeton, NJ: Princeton University Press, 1999.

Carpenter, Thomas H., and Christopher A. Faraone, eds. *Masks of Dionysus*. Ithaca, NY: Cornell University Press, 1993.

Cartledge, Paul. *Ancient Greek Political Thought in Practice*. Cambridge: Cambridge University Press, 2009.

Csapo, Eric, and William J. Slater. *The Context of Ancient Drama*. Ann Arbor: University of Michigan Press, 1994.

Davidson, John N. *Courtesans and Fishcakes: The Consuming Passions of Classical Athens*. New York: St. Martin's Press, 1998.

Eagleton, Terry. *Sweet Violence: The Idea of the Tragic*. Malden, MA: Blackwell, 2003.

Easterling, P. E., ed. *The Cambridge Companion to Greek Tragedy*. Cambridge: Cambridge University Press, 1997.

Else, Gerald F. *The Origin and Early Form of Greek Tragedy*. New York: Norton, 1965.

Euripides. *Euripides*. The Complete Greek Tragedies, vol. 4. Ed. David Grene and Richmond Lattimore. Chicago: University of Chicago Press, 1959.

Foley, Helene P. *Female Acts in Greek Tragedy*. Princeton, NJ: Princeton University Press, 2001.

Garland, Robert. *The Greek Way of Death*. Ithaca, NY: Cornell University Press, 1985.

———. *The Greek Way of Life*. Ithaca, NY: Cornell University Press, 1990.

Goldhill, Simon. *Reading Greek Tragedy*. Cambridge: Cambridge University Press, 1986.

Goldhill, Simon, and Edith Hall. *Sophocles and the Greek Tragic Tradition*. Cambridge: Cambridge University Press, 2000.

Gould, Thomas. *The Ancient Quarrel Between Poetry and Philosophy*. Princeton, NJ: Princeton University Press, 1990.

Grene, David, trans. *Sophocles 1*. 2nd ed. The Complete Greek Tragedies. Ed. David Grene and Richmond Lattimore. Chicago: University of Chicago Press, 1991.

Guthrie, W. K. C. *The Greeks and Their Gods*. Boston: Beacon Press, 1950.

Hanson, Victor Davis. *A War Like No Other*. New York: Random House, 2005.

Herodotus. *The Landmark Herodotus: The Histories*. Ed. Robert B. Strassler. New York: Pantheon Books, 2007.

Hughes, Bettany. *The Hemlock Cup: Socrates, Athens and the Search for the Good Life*. New York: Knopf, 2010.

Jebb, R. C., trans. *Electra*. By Sophocles. Cambridge: Cambridge University, 1894.

Kagan, Donald. *Pericles of Athens and the Birth of Democracy*. New York: Touchstone–Simon & Schuster, 1991.

Kells, J. H., ed. *Electra*. By Sophocles. Cambridge: Cambridge University Press, 1973.

Kirkwood, G. M. *A Study of Sophoclean Drama*. Cornell Studies in Classical Philology 31. Ithaca, NY: Cornell University Press, 1994.

Knox, Bernard M. W. *Essays: Ancient and Modern*. Baltimore: Johns Hopkins University Press, 1989.

———. *The Heroic Temper: Studies in Sophoclean Tragedy*. Berkeley: University of California Press, 1964.

Lefkowitz, Mary R. *The Lives of Greek Poets*. Baltimore: Johns Hopkins University Press, 1981.

Lloyd, Michael. *Sophocles: Electra*. London: Gerald Duckworth & Co., 2005.

Lloyd-Jones, Hugh, and N. G. Wilson. *Sophoclea: Studies on the Text of Sophocles*. Oxford: Clarendon Press, 1990.

Moore, J. A., trans. *Selections from the Greek Elegiac, Iambic, and Lyric Poets*. Cambridge, MA: Harvard University Press, 1947.

Pickard-Cambridge, Arthur. *The Dramatic Festivals of Athens*. 2nd ed. Revised with a new supplement by John Gould and D. M. Lewis. Oxford: Clarendon Press, 1988.

Plutarch. *The Rise and Fall of Athens: Nine Greek Lives*. Trans. Ian Scott-Kilvert. London: Penguin, 1960.

Radice, Betty. *Who's Who in the Ancient World*. London: Penguin, 1971.

Rehm, Rush. *The Play of Space: Spatial Transformation in Greek Tragedy*. Princeton, NJ: Princeton University Press, 2002.

Reinhardt, Karl. *Sophocles*. New York: Barnes & Noble–Harper & Row, 1979.

Seaford, Richard. *Reciprocity and Ritual: Homer and Tragedy in the Developing City-State*. Oxford: Clarendon Press, 1994.

Segal, Charles. *Sophocles' Tragic World: Divinity, Nature, Society*. Cambridge, MA: Harvard University Press, 1995.

———. *Tragedy and Civilization: An Interpretation of Sophocles*. Cambridge, MA: Harvard University Press, 1981.

Taplin, Oliver. *Greek Tragedy in Action*. Berkeley: University of California Press, 1978.

Thucydides. *The Landmark Thucydides: A Comprehensive Guide to the Peloponnesian War*. Ed. Robert B. Strassler. New York: Touchstone–Simon & Schuster, 1996.

Vernant, Jean-Pierre, ed. *The Greeks*. Trans. Charles Lambert and Teresa Lavender Fagan. Chicago: University of Chicago Press, 1995.

Vernant, Jean-Pierre, and Pierre Vidal-Naquet. *Myth and Tragedy in Ancient Greece*. Trans. Janet Lloyd. New York: Zone Books, 1990.

Whitman, C. E. *Sophocles*. Cambridge, MA: Harvard University Press, 1951.

Wiles, David. *Greek Theatre Performances: An Introduction.* Cambridge: Cambridge University Press, 2000.

————. *Tragedy in Athens: Performance Space and Theatrical Meaning.* Cambridge: Cambridge University Press, 1997.

Winkler, John J., and Froma I. Zeitlin, eds. *Nothing to Do with Dionysos?: Athenian Drama in Its Social Context.* Princeton, NJ: Princeton University Press, 1990.

Winnington-Ingram, R. P. *Sophocles: An Interpretation.* Cambridge: Cambridge University Press, 1980.

Zimmern, Alfred. *The Greek Commonwealth: Politics and Economics in Fifth-Century Greece.* 5th ed. New York: Modern Library, 1931.

ACKNOWLEDGMENTS

Translation is a thoroughly collaborative venture. The many scholars, theater practitioners, and friends who read and commented on this work at various stages deserve gratitude.

Three classicists, Thomas Fauss Gould, John Andrew Moore, and Charles Segal, did not live to see the publication of the present volume, but their influence and advice remains in the translations, introductions, and notes to the three Oedipus plays.

Mary Bagg's editing of the notes to this volume gave them clarity and accuracy they would not otherwise possess.

Thanks to the following readers for their contributions and suggestions: Normand Berlin, Michael Birtwistle, Alan L. Boegehold, Donald Junkins, Tracy Kidder, Robin Magowan, William Mullen, Arlene and James Scully, and Richard Trousdell.

Special thanks to my agent, Wendy Strothman, who saw the possibility of a complete volume of Sophocles and skillfully helped accomplish it.

ABOUT THE TRANSLATOR

Robert Bagg is a graduate of Amherst College (1957). He received his PhD in English from the University of Connecticut (1965) and taught at the University of Washington (1963–65) and the University of Massachusetts, Amherst (1965–96), where he re served as Graduate Director (1982–86) and Department Chair (1986–92). His awards include grants from the American Academy of Arts and Letters, the Ingram Merrill Foundation, the NEA and NEH, and the Guggenheim and Rockefeller foundations. His translations of Greek drama have been staged in sixty productions on three continents. Bagg, who is writing a critical biography of Richard Wilbur, lives in western Massachusetts with his wife, Mary Bagg, a freelance writer and editor.

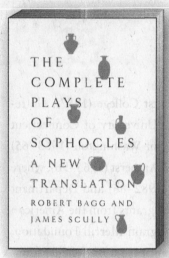
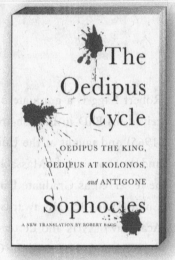